# ROUGH EDGE

## BROTHERHOOD PROTECTORS WORLD

## JEN TALTY

Twisted Page Press LLC

BROTHERHOOD PROTECTORS

ORIGINAL SERIES BY ELLE JAMES

*Brotherhood Protectors Series*
Montana SEAL (#1)
Bride Protector SEAL (#2)
Montana D-Force (#3)
Cowboy D-Force (#4)
Montana Ranger (#5)
Montana Dog Soldier (#6)
Montana SEAL Daddy (#7)
Montana Ranger's Wedding Vow (#8)
Montana SEAL Undercover Daddy (#9)
Cape Cod SEAL Rescue (#10)
Montana SEAL Friendly Fire (#11)
Montana SEAL's Mail-Order Bride (#12)
Montana Rescue (Sleeper SEAL)
Hot SEAL Salty Dog (SEALs in Paradise)
Brotherhood Protectors Vol 1

Rough Edge

Brotherhood Protectors
*Out of the Wild Series, book four*

*USA Today Bestselling Author*
JEN TALTY

*To Stacey Wilk. Thanks for finding the sweet spot!*

*All Sage Adams wants is for her parents take notice of her accomplishments. But when someone tries to kidnap Sage, she is forced to accept the ugly truth that her parents are criminals and it's now up to her to bring justice for all those innocent lives her parents have injured. However, she can't do it alone. Reluctantly, she teams up with Porter Clayton, a bodyguard from the Brotherhood Protectors.*

*Porter Clayton, better known as just Clayton, has never been ashamed of being the son of a whore. He's spent the last ten years of his life making sure his mother's work with helping prostitutes and their families make better life choices continues to grow. That had been the catalyst for him hiring Sage to plan a charity event. But when Sage ends up in the backseat of a hitman's car, Clayton will do whatever it takes to protect her.*

*Sage and Clayton must gather enough evidence to put her*

*parents in prison before Clayton is framed for a murder he didn't commit and Sage ends up dead. Working together, they come to terms with their past, their parents, and in the process they find the kind of love they hadn't even dared to dream could exist.*

# CHAPTER 1

SAGE ADAMS DIDN'T KNOW what was worse—having to sit across from the sexy, but still the son of a hooker, Porter Clayton, or the fact that her own father stood her up.

Again.

Talking a large gulp of her champagne, she glanced over her shoulder and then at her watch.

The charity event for the Alley Home had started three hours ago. Half the attendees had made their donations and had already left. A few drunk stragglers fumbled about the dance floor under the disco lights, determined to keep the party going. This event had been by far her biggest charity fundraiser and her most successful, in part thanks to Clayton showing up in honor of his mother and all she'd done in making the Alley Home happen.

She almost hadn't taken on the event because of what she knew about her father.

And a certain whore.

Sage shivered.

All she'd wanted was for her father to sit by her side and see all the good work she'd accomplished in the last couple of years.

But, as usual, her father couldn't be bothered. He didn't understand that the money she raised changed lives. Or that she didn't care about leasing a new Range Rover every three years. Hell, she was happy driving her Jeep, which her father had said had to be her second biggest mistake.

The first one had been when she'd gone into this line of work, to begin with. Her father didn't think very highly of those people who spent their days raising money and supplies for other people who should be doing whatever it took to rise up out of the hole they must have dug themselves into. Nope. Her dad was all about his bottom line.

His money.

Her mother wasn't any better. Actually, she was worse because she didn't even pretend to support Sage and anything she'd chosen to do over the years.

"Want another drink?" Weslynn Mayfair, her assistant, asked from her perch at the bar. Weslynn had been a godsend, working for very little while Sage got her charity event planning business up off the ground. Being a not-for-profit meant the salaries weren't high, but Weslynn didn't seem to care, often saying she'd do this kind of work for free if she didn't have bills to pay.

"Put them both on my tab." Sage dug into her purse and quickly sent a fifth text to her father, even though it appeared all the other ones had gone unnoticed or ignored.

Weslynn leaned in and gave her a big hug. "I'm sure something just came up."

"Something always comes up," Sage mumbled. Her entire life had been a series of events that were never important to her parents. Even when she'd had her appendix taken out while in Ireland for a summer, her parents didn't have time to visit, much less get her a plane ticket home. Nope. They called her twice while she was in the hospital, and that was it. No card. No flowers. No nothing.

"Hey, it could be worse. Your father could be like mine and show up wearing a dress, fake tits, and a beehive hairdo," Weslynn said.

"At least your father shows up. He cares for you, where mine only cares that I stay out of his and my mother's business." Sage resented the tremor in her voice. No one would ever describe her as timid or reserved.

She was the type of person who got shit done, and this event was something she was very proud of, and all she wanted was her father to rest his steady hand on her shoulder and tell her he was impressed.

Based on tonight, that wasn't going to happen.

Ever.

"You're overreacting," Weslynn said with a smile that could soothe a screaming baby.

"All my father cares about is how big his bank account is and if he has more cars than Jay Leno."

"You have a point there," Weslynn said as she waved down the bartender. "Another round, please."

Sage's phone buzzed. Quickly, she took a hopeful glance, but it was a weather warning, not a text from her father.

"You're coming out with me, right?" Weslynn cocked her right brow as she set a Cosmo down in front of Sage.

"I don't know. I've—"

"I won't take no for an answer. I got us an invite to an exclusive club." Weslynn turned her back. "Don't look now, but here comes sexy cowboy dressed in designer digs. Damn, that man is hot."

At this point, Sage wanted to kick off her shoes and soak her feet in a warm bubble bath. She wanted nothing to do with Clayton, as he preferred to be called. He waltzed across the room with a wicked-ass smile that reminded her of a rugged, shiftless cowboy in a field playing with cute puppies. She half expected a dog to be running up behind him like in one of those sexy beer commercials. He was the definition of tall, dark, and mysterious.

But he came from the streets and while he did good for the community, there was a dark cloud that hung over his head because of his mother. Didn't matter she'd managed to do some good with her life; she had died a prostitute, and that tainted the Alley Home.

One of the reasons she almost didn't take the gig, but Weslynn had talked her into it.

"Ladies." Clayton leaned against the bar. "When do we leave?"

"Leave?" Sage blinked.

"I invited him to tag along," Weslynn whispered.

"You did what?" Sage swallowed her pulse, but it bubbled right back up her throat, making her cough.

"She invited me to your after-hours party," Clayton said as he patted her on the back. He'd been pretty quiet during dinner, but she'd catch him staring at her, and it made her want to jump out of her skin. Not because he made her uncomfortable—well, actually he unnerved her—but it was because she kept picturing him shirtless walking a horse through a field of flowers.

But he was older, and his mother was still a hooker who had slept with her father.

"As what? A chaperone?" She hoped the snark would give him the hint she wasn't interested. She wasn't exactly sure how old Clayton was, but he was at least in his late thirties, if not older. Not that his age mattered to her in any way.

Clayton was one of those men who just seemed to get better and better with age, and damn, right now, he was about the hottest thing she'd ever laid eyes on.

He leaned in. His hot breath tickled Sage's cheek. "Are you even old enough to have that drink?"

"On that note, I'm going to use the little girl's room." Weslynn snagged her drink and scurried off like a rat leaving a sinking ship.

Figures. Weslynn had been trying to fix Sage up with just about every single man they encountered. Weslynn didn't seem to care if these men were close in age or even had the same interests as Sage. All that seemed to matter to Weslynn was that Sage hadn't had a man in her bed in over a year.

She cleared her throat and gave her chest a quick pound before bringing the martini glass to her lips. The vodka burned, but she didn't care. "I didn't mean to infer that you were old."

"I'm not that young anymore," he said with an amused twitch of his lips. "I couldn't help but notice that during dinner, we had an empty chair. Did your boyfriend stand you up?"

"That's an interesting way to ask if I have a significant other." She did her best to put on a breezy smile as if she didn't have a care in the world, but what she really wanted was to wipe that smug grin off Clayton's face.

"If you do, and he didn't show, he's an asshole." Clayton shrugged.

"If you must know, my date was supposed to be my father."

"Is he okay?" Clayton asked.

"He's fine. Just too busy to make an appearance."

"That's his loss," Clayton said with a sensitivity that surprised her.

"That doesn't change the fact he once again broke his promise." She had no idea why she hadn't just lied and told Clayton about some make-believe boyfriend who was a brain surgeon, and he had been called into work. Would have been less humiliating to have his pity over that than how he looked at her now with his warm eyes.

"I've never met your father, but I did meet your mom once." Clayton's smile faded. "You look exactly like her." He rested his hand on the back of her barstool.

"So, I'm told," she mumbled. "But I wouldn't know since I never see her." Shit, damn alcohol had gone right to her brain. "When did you meet my mother?" She shifted, making sure his hand didn't touch her bare shoulder.

Men like Clayton didn't travel in the same circles as her family, even though she knew for a fact her father often slummed with the very people the Alley Home tried to get off the street. But Sage found it hard to believe that her mother would spend any time with anyone from the Alley Home.

"It was years ago at a fundraiser for homeless children."

"That's my mom's go-to charity, but she doesn't often actually go to them. She just writes a check."

"As I recall, she wrote a hefty check but didn't stay long," Clayton said.

"Sounds like my mom."

"You've done some impressive things for a girl your age."

She rolled her eyes. "I'm not a child," she said under her breath.

"I can see that."

For the last four years, she'd busted her ass to make Adams Charity and Fundraising Foundation a success, but it had been an uphill battle between her parents telling her she was wasting her time and brain power and people like Clayton assuming she was too young and lacked the experience to pull it off.

"I wanted to thank you for putting this together. My mom would have appreciated your efforts." His words were kind, but his tone was strained, and what the hell did he mean by efforts? Was that just a phrase anyone would say? Was he just being polite? Was it a compliment? Or a diss?

"I don't have the final numbers, but we are close to having raised over a million dollars," she said, trying to keep her pride in check. "That should get your mother's educational center the supplies they need and then some."

His smile made her toes tingle.

"Money always helps, but that doesn't substitute the human touch, and the facility is sadly understaffed. I'm sure you noticed the chaos when you visited," he said.

"I haven't actually gone to the Alley Home. I hope that the money will help to add to the staff or anything else you and the board deem necessary." She wished she had the nerve to wave her hand dismissively as her father had always done when he'd finished with a conversation, but only because Clayton made her want to get out of her red dress and go skinny dipping with the sexy cowboy.

"In order to maintain a staff that way, you'd need to have this event every year. What we need are people willing to volunteer some of their free time. I'm trying to put together a program where high school students can help out and gain the necessary service hours they need to graduate, but I'm running into some blowback from the state education department."

She gulped her Cosmo. It burned her throat and made her eyes water. Where the hell was Weslynn? "I'm not surprised that the powers that be don't want to get involved in something like the Alley Home. It's not your typical shelter."

"No. It's not, but it's done more good than most and part of that is because the entire program is fed by Law Enforcement Assisted Diversion (LEAD) programs, and its sole purpose is to help prostitutes and their families make better choices and give them the opportunities they need to get off the street."

"You're not telling me anything I don't know. But you're never going to get the educational department to agree to accept service hours for their students when you have criminal activity coming and going almost daily." She knew the Alley Home did great things, but the concerns about criminal activity were real in the minds of the public since they didn't require abstinence from drugs or prostitution.

"Anything illegal isn't allowed inside or on the Alley Home campus," he said with his lips drawn in a tight line. "The police department works closely with those at the Alley Home, but because it's a voluntary program—"

"But anyone living in there or receiving services could be still be turning tricks, using drugs, or whatever else they've been doing on the streets." She'd read the mission statement and every article she could find on the Alley Home and its founder. She understood precisely how the educational facility worked and certainly didn't need a lecture from him. The Alley Home did excellent work. If it hadn't, she wouldn't have agreed to do this event. "It's not required of them to seek rehab or to stop selling their bodies altogether, so while the illegal actives might not be happening on the premises, nothing is preventing your clients from doing it."

"And that's kind of the point." He cocked his head. "These people are not a danger to themselves or society."

"I agree. But the education department and the conservatives in this community will fight that tooth and nail." She lifted her glass and took the last sip of her Cosmo, feeling the alcohol go straight to her head. Hopefully, when she stood, she wouldn't faceplant.

He raised his hands, palms toward the ceiling. "You're probably right on that. But be honest, what do you think? Do you find these programs offensive or effective?"

"For the most part, they are effective, but—"

"How do you know if you've never been inside one?" He stood, pushing back his coat and shoving his hands in his pockets. His eyes narrowed into a judgmental stare. "Have you ever been in a soup kitchen? Or hand out the last piece of chicken and there are still a dozen people in line, and two of them are children? Or how about—"

"No. I haven't. But I read the reports. I see the statistics. I've raised millions of dollars so that those things happen less and less." Wow. Nothing worse than being set up, and he'd set her up something good. He led her right down the path he wanted until she said the one thing that he could quickly pounce on, making her look bad. She knew his type all too well.

She stood and smoothed down the fabric of her red dress, adjusting the hem slightly, praying she didn't sway back and forth. "It's been a pleasure meeting you. I hope our paths cross again soon." She stretched out her hand. This night couldn't end quickly enough.

He took it in a firm grip and shook. "Until you visit the places you are trying to help, you have no understanding of what these people want or need."

11

The nerve of that man. "I don't need to spend a day there to know that those who walk through the front door need help, and the money I raise goes a long way." She scanned the room and found Weslynn leaning against the wall by the front door flirting with one of the waitstaff. "Take care, Clayton."

Sage snagged her clutch purse and on shaky heels, made her way across the deserted dance floor, keeping her chin up and not looking over her shoulder. Her heel caught against a wire that had been badly taped to the floor. She flapped her arms about like a wild bird, but all that did was hurl her pocketbook across the room.

Damn, this was going to hurt.

She pushed out her arms, bracing for impact when something substantial coiled around her middle and yanked her in midair.

"Whoa." She managed to brush her hair from her face while whatever held her set her feet on the ground, twisting her body. "Wait. I need to take these fuckers off." She kicked out of her shoes, not caring she just swore in front of...she glanced up. "Shit," she mumbled, staring into Clayton's pools of warm energy that were the color of the ocean when the sun beat down and showed the sand through the clear waters.

"Are you okay?" he asked.

"I'm fine, thank you. I just need to get myself into a Lyft."

"Are you going out to the club with your friend? Or heading home to Summerlin?"

She tilted her head. "What makes you think I live in Summerlin?"

"Isn't that where your parents live?"

She grunted, nodding her head. "But, for your information, I have my own place in Henderson." Well, her father owned numerous properties, so she didn't actually own it. That said, she hadn't lived with her parents since she had turned ten.

"Good for you."

She squinted her eyes. "What the hell does that mean? Another dig at my age?"

He raised his hands. "I'm just trying to have a conversation with you."

"It feels more like you're trying to figure out if I'm old enough to do my job. And for the record, I'm twenty-five. Not that my age makes any difference in my ability to raise funds, or to tell you to buzz off." For her entire life, she'd been justifying or defending her abilities, decisions, and choices in life to her parents. She sure as shit wasn't going to do it for a man who had needed her help to raise money for his project. She waved to Weslynn. "Are you ready to go, clubbing?" Sage hiccupped.

Oh boy, this was going to be a huge mistake.

# CHAPTER 2

CLAYTON COCKED his head and watched Sage's hips sway back and forth as she stomped across the dance floor in her bare feet. His heartbeat rattled his ribcage, and his breath got caught in his lungs.

She might be young, but she was all woman, and he found himself wanting to know more about her other than the fact she was a spoiled trust-fund baby. Granted, her skills at getting her wealthy friends to open their checkbooks and donate a shit-ton of money were out of this world. He'd never seen anyone work a room quite like she had.

He stuffed his hands in his pockets and strolled toward the door where she stood next to her assistant. He tried to tell himself that he was only interested in showing her what the Alley Home and places like it needed outside of the money. That statement was ninety percent true. The other ten percent was split between wanting to see her get her pretty little mani-cured hands dirty by spending a day volunteering and wanting to see what she looked like under that red strapless dress.

"Have you decided to come with us?" Weslynn asked with a bright smile.

He suspected that Weslynn was about the same age as Sage, but nowhere near as refined. He couldn't deny the fact that Sage was not only beautiful, but she was smart too.

And not just book smart.

She carried herself with a fair amount of confi-dence, but she still lacked the understanding that money only went so far. A concept that she was born into and part of Clayton wanted to show her reality.

But he wouldn't.

Or maybe he would.

Fuck. Women like Sage got under his skin in more ways than one. Her naivete over what her money and hard work did for those who needed it either came from her station in life, or her inability to see the truth.

He suspected it was the former, and that made him feel slightly better, but not enough so that he didn't want to set her straight.

The other problem with Sage wasn't really her problem, but his, because she was exactly his type in every way.

Except for maybe her age, but he had plenty of

friends who had wives and girlfriends ten or fifteen years younger.

Or older. Hell, Shamus, fellow Brotherhood Protector employee, his mother was something like twenty or thirty years younger than his father and not a single person on the planet would argue that those two were a perfect match.

Age was just a number.

Clayton knew that if he turned on the charm, they'd have a wild affair. It would be short-lived, but it would be one neither of them would soon forget.

"He's busy," Sage said, not glancing up in his direction.

"Last I checked I was a grown man capable of speaking for myself," he said with a hefty dose of sarcasm. She had a way of putting him on the defensive.

All while tying his gut up in knots.

Sage lifted her gaze, giving him the once-over. "Whatever you say, old man."

He tapped his chest. "That hurt, especially since I just kept you from kissing the floor with your pretty little nose."

She raised her index finger and rubbed her nose as she scrunched her face, giving him an odd look.

He handed the valet the keys to his pickup. "So, what club are you girls headed to?" His days of partying in Vegas ended when he left for the Navy twenty years ago. That thought reminded him of how young Sage was, only when he had been her age, he'd already finished his training to be a SEAL and had been deployed on at least a dozen special operations. That had been the most grueling thing he'd ever done in his life, and he remembered needing to run off some steam after every op, and that's probably what she was doing by heading to the clubs.

And he only wanted to spend a little more time with her, so, therefore, he could handle a club for one night.

"Are you seriously planning on joining us?" Sage asked.

"Absolutely." He grew up with hard knocks. He had to fight for every single thing he ever had.

She just had to ask daddy.

And yet, there he stood, staring, wanting to break his one golden rule.

Don't take the donors to bed.

"Have you ever heard of Dixie's Nightclub?" Weslynn asked.

He'd heard of and had been to just about every club on the strip back in the day. His mother's clientele sometimes consisted of rich men with a thirst for gambling and a good party, including Maxwell Busgy.

"I've been there. It gets a little too out of control most nights for my taste. You really might like the Firehouse better. It just opened a few months ago, and it's an—"

"Older, more mature crowd?" Sage asked as she

batted her lashes. They fluttered over her exotic eyes like butterfly wings in slow motion. "Is it like the mecca for the middle-aged?" Her voice took on a mocking valley-girl-type inflection.

He opened his mouth but slammed it shut. He supposed he deserved Sage's sarcasm, considering he accidentally insulted her age when he'd hit on her at the bar. "The Firehouse has a much better DJ lineup," he said.

"And you know this, firsthand?" Sage puckered her lips as if she'd just sucked on a lemon peel after taking a shot of tequila. "You've been there? I mean, don't you live in Montana or something?"

Well, he'd royally fucked up this conversation.

Actually, if he thought about it, she'd been the one to bring up the differences in age, so it was her that had the problem.

Not him.

And that sucked differently.

"A buddy of mine owns it, so I'm sure I could call him and get us a table if you'd like. Seriously, the club you are heading to has some major confrontations, and the cops are called every night of the week, not to mention it's in a shady part of town where drive-bys happen regularly."

Sage patted his biceps. "Thanks for the concern, but I've lived in Vegas my entire life, and the neighborhood Dixie's is in has gotten a lot better."

"Not really. The cops were there just last night." He

wanted to call her out on having lived in Vegas since her bio mentioned she'd been studying abroad since she was in the fourth grade.

"How do you know that? Where you there?" This time Sage's voice sounded more level and less like she wanted to stuff him in a trash can.

"I have a lot of friends who are cops." He'd been to one club this past week and not because he wanted to party, but because every once in a while, it was cathartic to remember where he'd come from. "Shall I call my friend at the Firehouse?"

"Sounds good to me," Weslynn said.

"I'm sure he has better things to do than hang out with a couple of kids like us," Sage said.

"Look," he said. "I'm sorry that I implied you were a child, which you are clearly not. My attempt at a pickup line failed miserably. Can we start over?"

Sage tossed her head back and laughed. "You've got to be kidding me. That comment about me being old enough to drink was you trying to pick me up? Damn, old man, you've lost your touch."

"You really think I'm an old man?" All the oxygen in his lungs escaped as if someone poked a hole in each one. It was slow, but it seemed impossible to fill them up again. "Because forty isn't old."

"No. It's not," Sage said, holding her phone up. "We'll try out the Firehouse. I need the address."

"That's a quick change of heart," he said, tapping the

address into her phone. "I have my car. I can drive if you want."

"I don't get into cars with strange men, young or old." Sage smiled, and if it were possible to actually knock someone's socks off, his would be across the street. She waved her phone in his face. "I've ordered a Lyft."

"That's getting in a stranger's car." He winked.

"That's different, and you know it." Sage slipped back into her shoes, holding his biceps for support. Her delicate touch tingled against his muscles. "Our Lyft is here. Who do I ask for when we get to the club?"

"Ronnie."

"We'll see you there, if you dare, old man." She pulled open the rear passenger door of a white four-door sedan. "Who are you picking up?"

Clayton smiled. Smart girl.

"Sage," the driver of the Lyft said.

She glanced over her shoulder. "Are you sure you're up for this?"

He hadn't a clue, but he didn't care. "Hell, yes."

"THAT COWBOY HAS to be the sexiest man alive."

Sage didn't disagree with Weslynn, but she wasn't going to say the words out loud. "He's okay to look at, but his personality is a little wonky."

"What the hell does wonky mean?" Weslynn asked

as she puckered her lips and brushed them with some gloss. "He's been trying to get your attention all night."

"I wouldn't go that far. Besides, you heard Clayton's so-called pickup line." She knew she looked more like twenty than twenty-five. Her mother always told her that when she was forty or fifty, she'd been grateful for looking younger. But now, all it did was make her behave as though she had a stick up her ass.

"He was trying to be cute," Weslynn said.

"It was creepy." That was a total lie. From him, the words sounded endearing and sexy, but she didn't allow those thoughts to linger in her brain for very long because she couldn't believe a man like him would be interested in a woman like her. Their worlds were a million miles apart.

His mother had always been present, even if she'd been a prostitute, where Sage's parents sent her off to boarding school because it was just too time-consuming to raise a child by themselves. She often wondered why her parents had a kid at all.

"You think he's hot," Weslynn said. "And I think you should go for it. When was the last time you had wild, out of this world, crazy sex?"

"None of your business." But the reality was the last time Sage had any sex had been months ago with a random guy she'd met at a fundraiser who turned out to be a class A liar. To make matters worse, the sex had been less than stellar.

She slumped back in her seat, closed her eyes, and took in a deep breath.

Weslynn rested her hand on Sage's thigh and gave it a good squeeze. "Stop thinking about your father. He's not worth it."

"I just wanted him to see what I've done and be proud of me."

"Oh, just stop," Weslynn said with a tinge of disgust. "You are the most well-put-together twenty-five-year-old I know. You've built this non-profit with your own two hands. You're nearing your final payment of paying your father back every dime you've borrowed; you pay your own bills, and—"

"I live in one of my parent's many real estate properties."

"You pay them rent," Weslynn said, shaking her head. "You know, with everything in your life other than your parents and romance, you are the most confident and smartest person I know. You don't need daddy's approval."

"It's not just about approval." All her life, she'd only wanted one thing, and that was to be part of something. She wanted to be part of a family. A real family. One where having a meal together was not an obligation used as a media stunt. "He didn't come tonight because he couldn't be bothered. This event doesn't do anything for him. Being here wouldn't have given my father anything but a headache."

"Perhaps. But remember, Clayton barely goes to any of the charity events your mom has been a part of."

Weslynn had a point, but Sage's mother hadn't created an entire foundation dedicated to raising money for social programs, diseases, or even disasters by the time she'd been twenty-three. Sure, her mother had a busy career as a corporate attorney, and Sage was very proud of her, but that didn't help fill the void created by not having her parents in her life. Her mom and dad left, raising a kid to nannies, schools, and summer camps.

"You're an amazing person. Now, let's go out and have a good time. We deserve it," Weslynn said.

The Lyft driver turned to the right.

He should have turned left.

Sage blinked her eyes open and sat up taller. "Excuse me," she said. "We're heading in the wrong direction."

"No. We're not," the driver said as he raised his arm. He held a small handgun in his grip.

Sage gasped and grabbed Weslynn's hand.

"What the hell is going on?" Sage sucked in a deep breath and forced her pulse to slow down as she tried to get a good look at the driver, but it was difficult sitting right behind him. In the review mirror, she caught a glimpse of part of his face, and he looked vaguely familiar.

Wait. Sage had seen the driver standing at the entrance of the club before they ordered their Lyft.

Shit. Could the driver have been waiting and listening to her conversation with Clayton?

"Where are you taking us?" Weslynn asked.

"You'll find out soon enough, so just sit back and relax," the man said.

Sage curled her fingers around the door handle and glanced over at Weslynn, who nodded.

*On three,* Sage mouthed. "What do you want with us?" Sage asked, waiting until the vehicle slowed before making a run for it.

The man laughed. "I don't want anything from either of you. I was hired to take you to a specific location, and that is exactly what I intend to do."

"Who hired you, and for what reason? Because kidnapping me won't get you a dime. My father cares more about his money than me."

"For our sakes, I hope that's not true," Weslynn whispered as she pulled out a small pocketknife.

Sage inhaled sharply. *One. Two. Three.*

Weslynn jammed the knife into the hand that held the gun.

*Pop!*

"Motherfucking bitch," the man said as the car swerved left, then right.

Weslynn slumped forward.

"No!" Sage reached in front of her friend and released the door before pushing Weslynn out of the car, Sage following only a couple of seconds later. Her body hit the pavement, and she skidded across the crushed gravel. She glanced up just as another car stopped only a few feet away. Her eyes stung, and the world around her blurred.

Just as the vehicle pulled out, another white sedan with the Lyft logo plastered on the dashboard rolled to a stop in front of him. He turned his head just as the car that Sage and her friend had gotten into braked at the light in front of the club. He leaned over and tapped on the window, making a mental note of the license plate of the other car.

"Who are you here to pick up?"

"Sage and that's not you," the driver said.

"Nope. I'm not." He jogged around the hood of the car and made his way toward his vehicle that the valet had pulled forward. He jumped in his truck, resting his cell on his lap. He punched the gas and skidded into traffic five cars behind the one Sage had gotten into, ignoring all the people shouting at him to slow down.

"Hey, Siri, call Hank Patterson." Clayton kept his gaze locked on the white sedan, making a right where it should have gone left.

"What's going on?" Hank's voice echoed out of the speaker on his phone.

"I'm following a car right now that I think is posing as a Lyft driver," he said calmly, something he'd always been notorious for. Calm under fire. His mother told him never to let anyone see him sweat, and he took that probably a little too literal.

"Why do you care about a Lyft driver?" Hank asked with a slight chuckle.

"I think Sage Adams was just kidnapped."

"You think?" Hank asked. "Because if I'm bailing you out of jail for any reason, you better be certain."

"Run this Nevada plate: GHJ 1125. I'm currently following the vehicle, and it's not going in the direction that Sage had planned on."

"Then why did she get into the car?"

Clayton pulled out into the left lane and passed two cars before making a sharp right. The vehicle he followed increased speed.

"She thought it was her Lyft. She did all the right things, but it wasn't her ride. They are headed out of Vegas and into a sketchy neighborhood. I'm going to cut them off at the pass. I've got some friends at the Las Vegas—"

"Do what you have to."

"I'm going to go. I'll call you when I have Sage safe and sound." Clayton knew Vegas and the surrounding areas like the back of his hand. At any given moment, he could close his eyes and visualize the entire city. He also knew that this particular neighborhood was under some major renovations, all trying to make it a safe place again.

He took a right and then two streets down he took a quick left, in hopes of cutting off the other car. When he pulled out onto the road, he had to slam on the brakes, so he didn't run Sage and her friend over as they leaped from the car.

Clayton jerked to a stop only a foot away from where Sage lay on the ground.

"Shit," he muttered as he raced toward Sage, her assailant taking off like a bat out of hell into the dark streets.

Sage raised on her hands and knees and started crawling toward her friend, who lay on the ground, blood pooling around her arm.

"Don't move." Clayton rested a firm hand on Sage's shoulder.

"He shot Weslynn." Tears rolled down Sage's face.

"Have you been shot? Are you hurt?"

She shook her head as she tried to stumble to her feet. "We have to help her."

"You stay here." He held out his cell phone. "Call, 9-1-1." He surveyed the area, making sure whoever had tried to harm Sage and her friend was indeed gone.

His pulse increased as he reached down and touched the side of Weslynn's neck. She had a weak pulse, and her skin had paled. He tugged off his sport coat before ripping up his shirt and using it to apply pressure to the wound. He soon realized that the bullet had gone right through her shoulder. He adjusted the fabric, covering both open wounds.

Weslynn opened her mouth, but all that came out was a gurgling noise.

The sound of sirens cut through the dense air.

"Is she okay?" Sage asked as she plopped herself on the pavement next to him. "Oh, Weslynn," Sage whispered.

Weslynn moved her mouth again.

"Don't try to talk," Clayton said. When he'd been in the military, Hank and Boomer used to tease him that he had very little emotion and that his inability to feel anything on a gut level might be useful in the field, but it wasn't going to help him outside of combat.

Especially when it came to women and relationships.

Well, he didn't do relationships, and he hadn't had a regular woman in his life in years. He was good with that, so why the hell did he need to feel anything? He glanced at Sage, who knelt by his side, holding her friend's hand. His heart beat a little faster. His breath hitched in this throat. Something about this woman turned his calm resolve into hyped adrenaline, and that was a feeling he did not welcome.

"Hang tight," Sage said, leaning over her friend. "Help is on the way."

"Did you know the driver?" Clayton asked.

"No. I don't think so." Sage shook her head. "How could I have been so stupid? I should have known he wasn't our driver."

"Don't beat yourself up. You followed all safety—"

"No, I didn't. That car didn't have the Lyft logo, but

I didn't notice that until it was too late. I won't be able to live with myself if something happens to her."

He kept the pressure on Weslynn's wound as he glanced up and caught Sage's gaze. "I've seen a lot of shit in the military, and your friend is going to be just fine."

"You can't be certain." Sage's voice shook.

The sounds of her shattered resolve squeezed at his heart. "It's a clean gunshot wound that went straight through."

"What do you know? You're not a doctor."

"Maybe not, but I've seen my share of bullet wounds, including having been shot five times myself," he said.

A paramedic truck rolled to a stop. Behind it was a fire engine, a cop car, and an unmarked vehicle.

"What happened?" a paramedic asked.

"Twenty-five-year-old female. A bullet wound to the shoulder. Decent pulse, but the right eye is dilated. Possible concussion."

"We'll take over from here," the paramedic said.

"Come on." Clayton tugged at Sage's arm when the paramedics took over Weslynn's care.

"I'm not leaving her side." Sage glared at him with wide eyes.

"Please, ma'am. We need you to back up and get checked out," one of the paramedics said.

Clayton bent over and lifted Sage into his arms. She

had a petite frame, at maybe five foot four, but her body was solid muscle.

"Put me down." She smashed her fist on his shoulder.

"Gladly, once we are out of the way." He nodded to one of the firefighters who waved him over. Gently, Clayton set her down on the back of the ambulance. Taking a step back, he let the EMT do his job.

"I'm fine," Sage said with a defiant quiver of her lower lip. "Everyone should be working on my friend."

"She's in good hands," the EMT said.

"Unbelievable. I get to see you twice in the same week?" a familiar male voice called. "How is it you always manage to find yourself in the middle of something?"

Clayton spun on his heels and smiled. There stood Detective Ryan Frost. As a beat cop, he was one of the first police officers to embrace Law Enforcement Assisted Diversion programs. One of his first clients had been Clayton and his mom.

Frost had also led up the investigation into who killed Clayton's mom, and while the case was still technically unsolved, the culprit was indeed behind bars.

"I can't seem to help myself," Clayton said with an outstretched hand. "How did you get here so fast?"

"I was in the area working another case when someone called about two women jumping from a car after hearing a single gunshot. Care to tell me how you're involved in all this?" Frost had to be pushing sixty, so it was a bit of a shocker that he was still on the job. But he mentioned that he'd rather die on the job than die a slow, boring death.

Clayton could relate to that concept.

"I was heading to the Firehouse to meet Sage and her friend when I realized they hadn't gotten into a Lyft, so I followed them. I took a side street to cut them off, but they had already been tossed from the car."

"For the record, we jumped. And the driver is wounded." Sage leaped from the back of the ambulance and lunged forward, stumbling over her own two feet.

Clayton raced to her side, catching her right before she managed to fall flat on her face. He held her to his chest and brushed her hair from her face. "We need to stop meeting like this."

"Not the time or place for stupid jokes," she mumbled. "I want to ride with my friend to the hospital."

"We need to ask you some questions," Frost said.

"Can't you do that at the hospital?" Sage asked.

"We could," Frost said. "But I'd rather do it now."

Clayton kept his arm around her waist to give her support on her wobbly legs. Her body shook, which was to be expected, considering what just happened. "I'll take you to the hospital, no problem." Clayton's phone buzzed. He glanced at the screen. "I've got to take this." He tapped the green button. "What's up, Maddog?"

"Hank got the owner's name of the car."

"And?"

"You're not going to like it," Maddog said.

"Just give me the name."

"Glenn Nolan."

"Fuck," Clayton mumbled. Nolan had spent some time in prison and was known as a freelance thug. No job too big or too small if the price was right and Nolan had done some work for Maxwell over the years. However, Nolan had a nasty habit of turning evidence over to the cops so he could cut a deal for a lesser charge. "Thanks for the intel." He stuffed his phone in his back pocket. "The owner of the car was Glenn Nolan."

"Jesus. We just picked him up last week, but since he gave up the supplier, we let him go. He's an elusive son of a bitch," Frost said. "And if his intel weren't always spot on, I'd toss the book at him."

"Playing both sides is going to get him killed."

"What's going on?" Sage asked. Her hand pressed against his chest as she glanced up at him with her sea-green eyes. "Who is this guy, and what does he want with me?"

"Do you know Maxwell Busgy?" Clayton wondered if this man would ever stop haunting him.

"Everyone knows who he is, but I don't know him personally. And what does he have to do with the man who tried to kidnap me?" Sage asked.

"I have no idea, but I intend to find out." Clayton

took Sage by the hand and tugged her toward his pickup.

"Where are you taking me?" Sage yanked her arm free.

"To the hospital. And on the way, you're going to tell me why the hell someone wants to kidnap you, Weslynn, or both of you."

# CHAPTER 3

SAGE TAPPED her foot while she waited for her father to pick up his damn phone.

"What do you need, Sage?" her father asked with his usually clipped tone that made her want to climb under a rock and never come out.

"Where are you?" It had been two hours since she'd spoken to her father. He should have been at the hospital an hour ago.

"At home. In bed. Trying to get some sleep, as you should be."

She sucked in the gasp that bounced from her gut to her throat like a game of ping pong. "I've been waiting for you. I thought you'd want to talk with Clayton or something." Or maybe hug your daughter, but that might be too much to ask.

"I've spoken to his boss. We've hired him to protect

you, but he should already know that. And don't give him any money; I've already taken care of his fee."

Of course, her father had. "I was hoping to see—"

"I've got a busy morning and so does your mother. I'll talk to you later."

The phone went dead.

Sage dropped her cell into her purse and let out a shaky breath. Her father would never change, and that was something she needed to come to terms with.

"Are you ready?" Clayton asked as he turned the corner, holding two cans of soda.

"I don't want to leave her." Sage paced in the hallway outside of Weslynn's recovery room. She had to have surgery on her shoulder, and she'd suffered a mild concussion, but the doctors assured Sage that Weslynn would fully recover.

"You heard the doctor. She's going to be sleeping for a while. It's almost three in the morning, and you need to take care of yourself as well." Clayton rested both of his hands on her shoulders, massaging gently. "Frost made sure to have a beat cop here at all times, and my buddy Maddog is on his way. He's one of the best in the business."

"My father and his money to the rescue." Her body defied her mind and relaxed into Clayton's tender touch.

"Your father might have paid for our services, but I'm the one who came to your rescue, and if you need it again, I'll be the one taking care of you, and I don't need a penny from anyone to do that."

She glanced over her shoulder and wrinkled her forehead. "No offense, but you sound like a Neanderthal."

"I suppose I do." He laughed. "We can come back tomorrow after you've gotten a few hours of sleep and a decent meal."

His fingers kneaded her tense muscles. She wasn't used to touchy-feely kind of people. Her parents weren't huggers. Hell, they barely shook hands with people. As a kid, she was starved for physical attention. As an adult, she'd learned to live without it. But that didn't mean she didn't still crave it.

And it was Clayton's attention she desired.

"I don't need a babysitter," she mumbled. What she wanted more than anything was for her parents to be actively engaged in her life, but instead, her dad did what he always did.

He hired someone to deal with his daughter.

"Well, good, because that's not what I am or what I do."

"I didn't mean it like it sounded." She stared at her aching feet. "Why can't we stay here?" She lifted her gaze and held her breath as she stared into the caring blue eyes of a man she barely knew, but who had affected her like no other. Her entire life she'd been emotionally on her own. Not once had anyone ever really been there for her, except for Weslynn. She'd become more than an assistant, and Sage wanted to make sure that Weslynn knew without a doubt that Sage would be there.

"Because we're both exhausted. We need a few hours of sleep and a decent meal. Then we need to talk through who could possibly want to kidnap you, or kill you, and why."

She closed her eyes and rubbed her temples. For the last two hours, she'd been racking her brain, trying to make heads or tails of what happened, but she came up empty-handed. She had very few real friends, but she had many acquaintances, both personal and professional, and to her knowledge, she got along with every single one of them. While she was known for getting things done and speaking her mind, she always believed she had done so respectfully and without too much conflict. Her work was all about helping people, and everyone she'd worked with so far had been grateful, and many were coming back to her to plan their next big fundraiser.

Her father, on the other hand...

She snapped her gaze back to Clayton. "What if they weren't after me?"

"Who then?"

"You must know what my father does for a living."

Clayton nodded. "I'm sure your father has many enemies, and that's something to consider, but right now, it's you I'm charged to protect, so I want to focus on that."

"I'd look into what business he's taken over in the last year and look at the men and women he's ruined in the process."

"My boss is looking into that, but again, you are my only focus right now."

If she hadn't seen her best friend get shot, she might think this whole bodyguard thing was over the top. "Have you spoken directly to my father?"

Clayton shook his head.

"He never called you?" She knew the answer, but she needed to hear Clayton's response.

"No. He called my boss, Hank. Why?"

"You would think my father would be more concerned with his only daughter," she said with a slight laugh. "I'm tired of my father substituting money for being an actual parent." Salty tears stung the corners of her eyes. She clenched her fists, desperately trying to push down the anger and sadness that burned her throat. "My entire life has been one one-hundred-dollar bill after the other. He couldn't be bothered to come to my high school graduation, so he bought me a car. For my college graduation, he bought me a condo to live in—in France, no less. But could he show his support by being there? God, no." As the words tumbled fast and furious from her lips, she watched as Clayton opened and closed his mouth at least five times. She knew she should shut the hell up, but this had been bottled up inside her gut for so long, it was as if a tidal wave had taken over. "His idea of being a good parent is to make sure someone else is taking care of me, so all he's ever done is write a check. It's how he handles everything because to him; money is love."

Clayton reached out and tipped her chin with his thumb and forefinger. His gaze tore straight to her heart.

She gasped.

"I'm truly sorry your family isn't here for you right now, but I have a job to do, and honestly if your father hadn't hired the company I work for, I would have done it for free."

"Why would you do that?" she asked, swiping at her face.

"Because I wouldn't be able to walk away knowing someone might try to hurt you again," Clayton said as he wrapped his arm around her waist and led her toward the elevators. "Now, let's go back to your place. We can stay there tonight, but I think we'll need to move to a hotel or something tomorrow. Glenn Nolan is bad news, and he used to work for the man who I believe killed my mother."

"What?" She stopped dead in her tracks and shoved her finger in her ear. She couldn't have heard that correctly. She knew his mother had been killed and that her murder went unsolved. There were a dozen different stories that milled about the water coolers in this town about how she died and who killed her.

One of which had been Maxwell Busgy.

"So, this could be about you?" She took a step back, giving herself some distance.

"I wasn't the one who was kidnapped, so I don't think so."

"But you have enemies, and one of them is Maxwell Busgy, so he could be trying to get to you. I mean, tonight was about honoring your mother and her work with the Alley Home."

"But I hadn't announced my attendance until the day before the event." The elevator doors swung open, and six people hurried past them. She adjusted her strapless dress in a nervous attempt to calm herself down. Her mind went to a million different places. Her heart hammered in her chest. Nothing like this had ever happened to her before. "Let's not forget the fake Lyft driver said your name."

"But still, maybe—"

"I have enemies, and yes, one of them is Maxwell, but he's behind bars, and I helped put him there." Clayton reached out and curled his long, thick fingers around her biceps. "If Maxwell sent someone for me, and I didn't see him coming, I'd be dead. I know that. But I wasn't the one who was almost kidnapped. You and Weslynn were. I know you're scared and confused. But trust me, I won't let anything happen to you, and my buddy, Maddog, won't let anything happen to your friend. I promise you that we will do whatever it takes to ensure your safety."

"Anyone ever tell you that you're a bit too serious?"

Clayton let out a slight chuckle and smiled. "You're not the first one to tell me how detached I come across. I can't help it. Between how I grew up and my training as a SEAL, I learned to keep my emotions in check. I've managed to stay alive in some dangerous situations because of it." He laced his fingers through hers and tugged her into the elevator. "But make no mistake, I love my job, and I care about human life."

"Jesus, you sound like that weirdo half-human guy from Star Trek."

"At least I don't look like Spock." Clayton had the nerve to wink.

But what truly mortified her was the fact her lips tipped up into a smile. "Anyone ever tell you that you're utterly impossible?"

"My mother used to tell me that every day."

Sage glanced down at their intertwined hands. His thumb ran up and down her finger. His skin felt warm, and his grip made her feel safe. Everything about this man turned her upside down and inside out. He put new meaning into the word: an oxymoron.

Silence filled the small space. All she could hear was the pounding of her heart. Cobwebs filled her mind. Her thoughts clung to the strings, unable to break free. Perhaps that was for the best. Clayton was right. She was exhausted, and collapsing in her own bed for a few hours would give her the reboot she needed to figure out what the hell had happened this evening.

They headed out of the hospital and into the

parking garage, hand in hand. Part of her knew she should pull away, but the other part needed his strength. Not to mention she'd almost fallen on her face twice tonight. A yawn gripped hold of her chest, and she nearly fell asleep leaning against the hood of his truck as he pulled open the door.

"Up you go." He lifted her into his arms and set her gently in the passenger side of his massive pickup. The plush leather seats conformed to her body.

"Thanks for being here for me when my father was too busy to make an appearance."

"I'm nothing like your father." He cupped her face with his big, powerful hands. His gaze held her captive, and her heart thumped into the back of her throat. "I'm probably stepping out of turn here, but your father is an asshole."

"What sucks is that it's taken me this long to realize he doesn't give a shit about me, only how I make him look."

"You're not defined by your parents."

"Do you really believe that? I don't mean to be insulting, but your mother was a hooker, and I'm sure people have made judgments about you because of it."

He nodded. "Growing up, people thought my mother didn't love me simply because she was a prostitute. How could a woman who sold her body for money love a child if she couldn't love herself? Only, most whores go into the prostitution world kicking and screaming. They tried to survive other ways, but the money is too good, and then it just becomes nearly impossible to get out."

"What your mother did doesn't bother you?"

"My mother had me when she was only seventeen. She was young, scared, and alone. All she knew was selling her body for money. It might sound crazy, but she continued the lifestyle in part because she loved me. She would do anything, and I mean anything, to ensure I had food in my stomach and a clean place to live. When she tried regular jobs, we ended up on the streets or in shelters, but when she worked as a prostitute, we had enough money to more than survive."

"You skirted my question."

"Of course, it bothered me, but I don't judge her for her decisions."

"But she chose to continue to do something illegal even after she'd started the Alley Home, which put her turning tricks and the money above you." She covered her mouth. Why Clayton made her go all loose in the lips was beyond her. She wasn't even tipsy anymore.

Clayton reached across her and fastened her seatbelt before slamming the door shut and jogging around the back of the vehicle. He climbed behind the steering wheel.

"Just because our parents do things we can't understand, or aren't the touchy-feely kind of parent, doesn't mean they don't love us," Clayton said as he backed out of the parking spot. His attention focused everywhere but on her.

Story of her life.

"I don't think my parents understand love." Perhaps that's why she hadn't ever been able to fall in love.

The sound of tires squealing to a stop caught her attention. She glanced over her shoulder as a black sedan came flying around the corner.

"Get down," Clayton said calmly as he pushed her head to her lap and rammed the gearshift into drive. "Stay low and hold on to something."

"What is—"

*Pop!*

She screamed, trying to lift her head, but he kept his hand over it.

He punched the gas and sped forward. The vehicle pitched left, then right, and then her body jerked forward as he raced right through the gate.

"Hey, Siri, call Maddog," Clayton said as if nothing terrible had just happened.

"What's up, man?" a deep voice boomed through the vehicle's speaker system. "I'm about to take off."

"We just got shot at leaving the hospital. I need you to call Frost and let him know. It was a dark sedan. Nevada plates that start with 8F9, but I didn't get the rest. I seem to have lost them, but I'm going to take a weird way to get to my old stomping grounds where I left my trailer. Do you have the address?"

"Sure do," Maddog said. "Guess our bad guys don't have very good aim."

"Didn't even hit my truck. I think it was supposed to scare us." Clayton took a sharp turn.

"It scared the hell out of me." Her body slammed against the door. Once again, she tried to sit up, but he kept her head pushed between her legs.

"It would scare any normal person," Maddog said. "But our friend Clayton is far from normal. I bet his heart is barely beating."

"My pulse is elevated, just for the record."

"Not sure that makes me feel better," she mused.

"We gotta go. I'll be in touch," Clayton said. A few seconds later, the call was replaced with a song from the Rolling Stones.

Her chest hurt every time she tried to suck in a deep breath. She buried her face between her knees, staying as low as she possibly could. Fear seized her heart. Nausea grabbed hold of her stomach and churned until it soured.

"Just breathe," Clayton said, his fingers kneading the back of her head. "I want you to stay down just a little while longer."

She opened her mouth, but all that came out was some strange noise that sounded like a dying cow. Minutes ticked by as Clayton took one sharp turn after the other until he sped up.

"We won't be going back to your place now." He let go of her head.

She swallowed a small amount of bile that bubbled up from her gut. Sitting up tall, she glanced around.

Clayton weaved in and out of traffic on the high-way. She leaned over, surprised to see he wasn't speeding.

"Where are we going?" she asked with a rattle in her vocal cords. Right now, having his level voice wouldn't be a bad thing.

"A place I know where we'll be safe."

"I think I might be safer on my own," she mumbled.

"Trust me. If I thought that were true, I'd be drop-ping you off at the next restaurant."

That certainly didn't make her feel better. "I don't understand what's going on. This makes no sense to me. I'm a good person. I can't imagine why anyone would want to hurt me." Sage clutched her chest when her cell phone buzzed. She dug into her purse and pulled it out. She stared at the screen with her mouth hanging open.

"Who is it?"

"My father," she said softly. "Why is he calling me? An hour ago, he practically hung up on me."

"Answer it."

She swallowed her breath and hit the green button. "Daddy?" While she spoke with her father regularly, it was rare he called her first.

"Where are you?"

Clayton shook his head.

"I'm not exactly sure," she said, doing her best to refrain from being sarcastic.

"I bet that guy from the Brotherhood Protectors

told you to say that," her father said. "But I need to know where you are."

"He doesn't think that's a good idea."

"Put him on the phone."

"You're on speaker," she said half under her breath. For a split second, she thought about telling dear old dad about being shot at again, but she decided the only thing that would accomplish was to remind her that her parents saw her as an appendage they were responsible for, but not as their daughter. Not as a flesh and blood human being that needed hugs and the occasional pat on the back.

Who was she kidding? Her parents didn't even do that, and she figured their marriage was more out of convenience than out of love.

"I'll cut right to the chase," her father started.

Clayton glanced in her direction with an arched brow.

She shrugged her shoulders.

"A couple of months ago, I took over a company called Rotork. It was a family-owned business that years ago did quite well. Unfortunately, the company took a downhill turn, making it ripe for someone like me to come in and—"

"I'm sorry, sir, but could you cut to the point," Clayton said with a sharp edge. He gripped the steering wheel with both hands.

"I'm getting there. I think the backstory is important."

"Not when I'm trying to outrun a bad guy with a gun."

She liked the way Clayton handled her father.

"Jonathon Rotork, the son of the founder, told me when I sold off the company for parts that he'd make sure I paid, and just the other day, when I ran into him at a coffee shop, he told me to watch my back. I think he's your guy."

"Send any and all information to my boss, and we'll look into it." Clayton reached out and squeezed her thigh. "I'll take good care of your daughter."

The phone went dead.

"Love you too, Dad," she said, resting her head against the glass. "The scary part is the apple doesn't fall far from the tree."

"Trust me; you're nothing like your father." Clayton left his hand on her leg.

She should brush it off, but she decided she liked the human contact, even if it was from Mr. Calm-Cool-And-Collected.

# CHAPTER 4

CLAYTON CONSIDERED himself a good judge of charac-
ter, but he wasn't so sure what to think of Sage. There
was no denying she was one smart filly. What she'd
accomplished with her foundation was truly amazing
between charity events like last night, or providing
needed aid to disaster zones, without even being asked.

He adjusted himself in the folding chair and stared
into the crackling fire as flames flickered in the early
morning light. Sipping his coffee, which was more like
grinds mixed with hot water, he stared at his camper.

His home.

Hank and Swede had burst out laughing when he
pulled into Hank's place in Eagle Rock, Montana, six
months after his mother died and only three weeks
after he'd retired from the military. Hank had offered
him a cabin to rent until he got a place of his own, but
Clayton already had a home, and it went with him

wherever he went. His mother always told him never to have more possessions than you can pack up and move in less than a few hours. He'd taken that advice literally, but it was also what he'd become accustomed to. He and his mother went from one shelter to the next when he'd been a small boy. Then she met Maxwell and that had been both a blessing and a curse.

And in more ways than one.

"Clayton!" Sage's scared voice cut through the dense Nevada air.

He jumped to his feet and flipped open the door to his fifth wheel trailer. "I'm right here."

"Where the hell is here?" She stood between the kitchen and the bedroom in one of his button-down shirts, the hem flowing loosely over the top of her knees. Her dark hair fluffed out over her shoulders in a wild morning look.

He swallowed. "Welcome to my humble abode."

"Excuse me?" She blinked, brushing her hair from her wide eyes. "Where exactly are we?"

"Boulder Beach Campground," he said with a slight smirk. He shouldn't enjoy playing with her, but it was too much fun to pass up.

"You live in Montana."

"I live in this camper, regardless of what state I'm in." He raked a hand across his buzzed head. Instead of giving her short answers, he should just lay it out there, but again, the look on her face was priceless.

"You've got to be kidding me? What are you; some kind of nomad?"

"Pretty much." He took her by the hand and tugged her toward the kitchen. "The coffee tastes like shit, but I have fresh eggs and bacon. Let me cook you breakfast."

"I want to check on Weslynn."

"She's fine. My buddy Maddog is with her, and she's awake. They are keeping her a couple more days and then releasing her." He squeezed her hand and smiled. "No one has tried to come near her."

"I still want to go see her and grab some clothes. Can I take your truck?"

He placed both his hands on her biceps. "Sweetheart, you and I are stuck together for a while, so you might as well get used to it. Now, I don't have any clothes that will fit you, but Frost is going to be stopping by some time with some clothes, so until then, feel free to rummage through my drawers for something that might come close to fitting, or stay in this." He took a step back and let his gaze drop to her sexy pink toenails. As if she knew he found them utterly adorable, she wiggled them. "Because you look damn hot." Did he just say that out loud?

"Do you always stare at the women you protect like their pieces of meat to be devoured?"

He laughed. "Babe, you are no slab of beef, and I wouldn't devour you. It would be more like savoring every inch of you." He dropped his hands to his sides.

He'd never had trouble getting a woman into his bed when he wanted one, which wasn't all that often. When he did approach a lady, he was almost always confident that they were relationship phobic.

But Sage? She was the kind of woman who would want a man, not because she needed him, but because she wanted someone to share her life with—a true partner.

And Clayton had no idea what that meant, nor did he want to find out.

Or did he?

He let his gaze slide up her tanned legs, across the white shirt covering her perky, braless breasts, to her lower lip, which she bit down on in a sexy, contemplative look.

"That was insanely inappropriate of me, but for the record, had I not been hired to protect you, last night I would have worked my best charm to see you in my shirt after a night of wild, passionate lovemaking."

She covered her mouth and laughed.

And laughed.

She laughed so hard he wondered if she was crying too. Or maybe just gasping for air.

He stood there like an idiot waiting for her to stop. He might be a man of few words but never had a woman rendered him utterly speechless. "I honestly don't see what's so funny."

She waved her finger in the air. "You don't seem like

the type of guy who would ever use the words *lovemaking*."

The corners of his mouth tipped upward. She had a point. "And what do you think I would say?"

"Oh, I don't know, maybe a night of wild sex?" She lifted her palms toward the ceiling. "Oh hell, I see you saying, let's fuck over anything else." Her nose scrunched when she used the swear word.

"I might have a bit of a rough edge to me, but I'm still a gentleman."

She rested her hand on his chest and tapped.

His skin tingled from his head to his toes. The last time he felt like this had been when he lost his virginity.

"All right then. I'll take some breakfast. Mind if I shower while you cook?"

"Be my guest." He took her hand and pressed his lips against her palm.

"Where's my phone?"

"Shut off in the glove box of my truck. For the time being, you're offline. The best way for me to keep you safe while the cops and my buddies work on solving why Glenn Nolan tried to kidnap you."

She cocked her head and pursed her lips. "You said he worked for Maxwell, who you believe killed your mother, so why me? It still doesn't make sense."

"Nolan is a freelance thug. He works for anyone who pays him. If someone offered him enough cash, he'd kill Maxwell and not think twice. If Maxwell offered more not to be killed, he'd take the money and let Maxwell live. So, the questions we need to be answered are: who hired him and why?"

She yanked her hand free.

His skin immediately cooled. The damn woman had made her way into his bloodstream in a single night.

"I hope we find those answers by sunset because I don't want to spend a full night out here in this thing. Besides, I have a flight to catch, and I am going to need to get ahold of some of my staff to give them directions on what to do."

"You can use my phone later, but you can't tell anyone where you are or why. Now scoot and get that shower." He turned her body and patted her butt. Shit. So much for being a gentleman.

She glanced over her shoulder. "You're lucky you're so pretty," she said before disappearing into the entranceway to where the bedroom and bathroom were located.

He wasn't quite sure how to take her statement, but at least she hadn't responded with a slap across the face. His phone buzzed in his back pocket. He glanced at the text from Hank telling him to check his email ASAP.

The sound of water rushing through the pipes filled his ears. His mind immediately went to her tight nipples that had pressed up against his white shirt. He hoped he'd gotten her bra and clothing sizes correctly.

He rolled his eyes. If he got them right, she'd probably be just as insulted as if he hadn't.

Snagging the frying pan, he fired up the stove. He wasn't much of a cook, but he could handle plain scrambled eggs and bacon. The bacon sizzled, and the grease jumped out of the pan and smacked his arm. He welcomed the sting because it replaced the warm, fuzzy feelings that stirred deep in his soul.

He understood love, but other than his mother, he'd never really experienced it. Sure, the men and women he worked with he had strong feelings for. Hell, he'd die for any one of them.

But the kind of love that Maddog and Jolie had? Or Shamus and his wife? That kind of love was a concept that Clayton didn't believe he'd ever experienced, and that was fine by him. Love complicated things, and he liked his life nice and simple. No strings and if he ever got bored with the Brotherhood, he could up and leave.

He laughed as he flipped the bacon and added in the eggs. He'd been with the Brotherhood Protectors for ten years now, and he still wasn't bored. Not even close.

After putting all the food on two different plates, he set them on the table and flipped open his laptop. His mail icon bounced. One message from Hank. He clicked on it.

*Hey Clayton,*

*We got a hit on the partial plate. A holding company owns it and get this; the holding company is owned by Stanley Adams. I've attached some information on Stanley, his wife, their business, and some of their latest deals. This man has a lot of enemies, and he's been threatened before. But what's even more disturbing is he had dealings with Maxwell Busgy.*

*Call if you need anything.*

*Hank.*

CLAYTON SEARCHED his memory regarding his one phone call with Sage's father. Had he told them where he planned on taking Sage? No. The only people who knew were Hank and the rest of the team, and they wouldn't give up Clayton's location. Even so, it might be a good idea to head to a different campground.

He scanned the rest of his emails, but there was nothing that needed his attention now. He clicked on the first attachment, which was a picture of Maxwell standing in front of a building with his arm draped over Stanley's shoulder. Shit.

"Hey, Siri, call Hank Patterson."

The phone rang once. "I take it you got my email."

"I thought I knew every business associate Maxwell had." Clayton had a bad feeling in the pit of his gut when it came to Sage's father. His mother might not be winning any mother of the year awards, but she did her best to keep Clayton protected from the insanity of being on the streets.

"We both know that Maxwell had more than one legit business along with partners. On the surface, Stanley looks clean."

His mother used to tell him that almost nothing was as it seemed. One of her many life lessons, which included keeping his emotions bottled up inside. If you must cry, do it in the shower. Or late at night when you're all alone. She would tell him that showing any sign of weakness would permit people to take advantage of him.

The last time he cried had been the day he buried his mother, but it hadn't been at the cemetery. Nope. That would have upset his mother. So, he waited until he was in the privacy of his hotel room. That night, he cried for what seemed like hours.

To this day, he wasn't sure what he missed because, for most of his youth, he'd been raised by a group of hookers and their friends. His mother spent more time turning tricks than she did spending time with him. And then when things turned for the better, she spent all her time escorting Maxwell and his cronies around.

Then along came Frost after Maxwell had beaten her so badly, she ended up in the hospital. That had been the beginning of a new life.

Clayton had been fourteen. He thought that he'd get more time with his mom, but she jumped right into working at a shelter and eventually opening her own educational center. And Clayton still spent most of his time with prostitutes.

"Smells delicious out here." Sage sashayed across the floor, smelling of pine and wearing a pair of his boxers and one of his white V-neck shirts, tied at her hip. Her long, wet hair left damp spots in places that needed to be covered.

He cleared his throat as he pulled back the chair next to him and shoved a hot cup of what he hoped was better tasting coffee across the table. "How was your shower?'

"Fine, but how the hell do you fit inside that tiny little thing?"

"Very carefully," he said with a slight laugh.

"Wow. You have a nice smile. You should do it more often."

"I don't usually have much to smile at." His cheeks started to hurt from grinning wider than he'd done since he was a small boy. "But you seem to bring it out in me."

She reached out and traced her finger across his cheek. "Now, all we have to do is work on how you talk to people, and there might be hope for you after all."

"What does that mean?"

"The tone of your voice is distant. That's not who you are. You're tender and kind."

He groaned. "It's never a good idea to do this, but I've been thinking about it since I first saw you yesterday from across the ballroom." He cupped her chin, tilting her head.

She pressed her finger against his lips. "You aren't going to kiss me right now."

"Why not?"

"First reason is that I'm starving. But the more important reason is I want to know why you have a picture of my father with Maxwell Busgy displayed on your screen?" She tapped the computer and gave him a twisted smile.

"Are you sure you've never met him?" Clayton figured it was for the best she put the brakes on. She was his client, and while many of his buddies meet their spouses in similar situations, he wasn't looking for anything but a fling.

And she wasn't fling material.

She shook her head at the same time as she bit down on her lower lip.

He hated it when people lied to him, but for now, he wasn't going to push.

"Since I was ten, I've lived in boarding schools and summer camps, only coming home for Christmas. I went to college in New York City and worked summers up there. I've only moved back to the area in the last few years, and I can't say I've ever met anyone either of my parents works with."

"That didn't answer my question." Clayton scratched the side of his face. Her childhood sounded empty and sad, and the lines that etched deep in her forehead as she spoke about it let him know that she too felt a hole in her heart and a void in her soul. "Have you ever worked for your father? Remotely or in person? Even if it was only for a short time."

"Nope. My father told me that I needed to go out and make my own way in the world, although I don't think he wanted me to create a foundation, and he wouldn't have given me a job if I begged. He's decided his world isn't for me."

"I'm surprised. Most parents want their children to follow in their footsteps."

"Did your mother want you to follow in hers?" she asked with an arched brow, which she quickly retracted. "That was rude."

"I won't argue with you on that point, especially since I'm very proud of what my mother accomplished in her last years on this earth." Not once had Clayton been ashamed of being the son of a whore, and that was still true. But it didn't mean that comments like that didn't stab him in the heart. "Your mother is a successful lawyer and works with your dad, so I suspect his reasoning for keeping you from the family business is either because he's doing something illegal or he thinks you're incompetent."

"I hate to admit it, but he thinks I'm incapable of most things." She waved her finger near his face. "You think my dad's a criminal, don't you?"

"It's looking that way." He contemplated how much he should tell her about what Hank dug up, but he needed more time to process the information. "What about your mother? Does she support you?"

"About the same as my dad. They aren't warm, fuzzy parents."

"I guess not," he mumbled. His mother always showed him affection, showering him with hugs and kisses, but even that didn't make up for the fact that he could go days without seeing her, especially as a young man since many of her johns were wealthy businessmen who took her away for a week or two. "Can I ask you a personal question?"

"Sure." She shrugged, stabbing her eggs with a fork.

"Why haven't you ever been to the Alley Home?"

She dropped her utensil and coughed.

"Have you been to any shelter or disaster zone you've raised funds for?" he asked, knowing full well she hadn't.

"No. I haven't, and I take it you want to know why?"

"What you do is great, but it's not any different from writing a check. Money only gives people so much. Without a caring staff who are willing to go the extra mile, all the money in the world isn't going to solve the problems. You could bring awareness just by showing up."

She popped a piece of bacon in her mouth and stared at the ceiling. "I get what you're saying because I feel like my father thinks everything should be handled with donating money versus doing anything about it. But to answer your question, I don't go because I honestly don't have the time. But I do send my staff, and they report back. That's how I know where I want to put my energy."

Something in the way she avoided eye contact told him she was hiding her real reason, but he wasn't about to call her on it, just yet.

She shifted in her seat, tucking her feet under her butt. "My turn to ask a personal question. Have you ever been with a prostitute?"

He snapped his jaw and narrowed his eyes. "Why do you want to know that?" It hadn't been the first time someone had asked him that question, but it always took him off guard.

"Before I was shipped off to my first boarding school, I heard my parents fighting, which they didn't often do, but my mother mentioned something about some whore my dad had been with, and if she ever found out again, she'd ruin him."

"That's a lot for a sheltered little girl to deal with." He reached out and pushed her damp hair over her shoulder, gently running his fingers across her soft neck. "Do you know if your father still has a taste for hookers?"

"You say that so flippantly, which confuses me since your mother was…" She let out a long sigh. "I keep putting my foot in my mouth, don't I?"

He patted her knee. "Most people do."

"When I first started my foundation, I told myself I

wouldn't help prostitutes because of my father. I know he's cheated on my mom many times."

"That sucks. I'm sorry," he said with tightness in his throat. When he'd first met Sage, he struggled between the woman he knew her to be and the rich young lady who had yet to experience life.

Only, he'd been wrong. She had a shit-ton of experiences that tore at her heart and perhaps hardened her a tad, but it also left her misguided and full of fear, which surprised him.

"Are you asking me if I've been with a hooker to understand your father?"

She nodded.

He appreciated her honesty and wished he had the answers she was looking for. "I've never paid a woman for sex, but I don't judge the women who sell themselves. I do, however, resent the men who abuse them. Finding employment that pays the bills for many of these women isn't an option. They do what they have to in order to survive."

"Not all of them. I did my research on your mother, and she became a high-priced call girl—"

"Babe, I'm going to stop you there," he said, running his hand up her arm. "Men might have paid a hefty sum for her, but she didn't get most of that money. She didn't get to keep the gifts. Those all went to Maxwell. He controlled her until she found a way to steal from him, and even then, for whatever reason, she couldn't leave him."

"But not all women have pimps or whatever you call them. I've read articles about madams and other people who run brothels."

"Brothels are legal in some places in Nevada, and they are generally a very different beast, but for the most part, there is always someone who controls the prostitutes, and they often end up beaten, broken, or dead."

She opened her mouth, but he quickly shushed her.

"If you're going to say they deserved it or was asking for it, I'm going—"

"You really think that low of me that I would think anyone deserves that? Of course, they don't. I'm just telling you why I have an issue with prostitution and why I haven't gone to many shelters."

He pinched the bridge of his nose. "That's not why you don't go. I remember all the food, water, and necessities you managed to fund for the hurricane that hit the Panhandle last summer, but there wasn't a single picture of you at the disaster area."

"So? Why do I have to be there?"

"You don't, but at least be honest with why you don't go."

"Oh, and you have an opinion on the matter, don't you?"

He might as well speak his peace. "As a matter of fact, I do." The last thing he wanted to do was hurt her feelings in any way, but she didn't need him to coddle her or try to placate the situation. She needed to face the truth of her reality. "If you go, it will make it too real, just like why you don't want to be in the same room with a prostitute and deep down, you know once you start doing that, you're the kind of person who gets her hands dirty, and that scares you."

She sucked in her lower lip and bit down on it.

"You care deeply, but you're terrified if you get too close to anyone or anything, you'll get hurt because that's what your parents showed you, so you remain detached, even though you go one step further than your parents. You raise money instead of writing a check, but you refuse to get into the trenches because if you do, it means you'll see your life differently. Your parents differently." He tapped the small space between her breasts. "You have a big heart, but you've pressed it down into the depths of your soul, keeping you from really seeing and feeling for the people you are trying to help. Again, that would make it too real, and sadly, your parents only showed you that money means you care, only they don't care at all."

She shook her head and laughed. It wasn't a ha ha laugh, but it wasn't sarcastic either. It sounded more like his words struck a chord, and she was about to let reality bubble to the surface. "And did your mother care about you? I'm sorry, but I struggle with your mother's life choices, especially after she started the Alley Home."

He shrugged. "I'm no different. My mom might have been warm and loving, always showering me with hugs and kisses, but she never had time for me. She had to go out and make money so that I could have a better chance. And she gave me that, but it did come at a price." His heart beat erratically.

She tapped his chest. "That price was what it did to you, and don't tell me that you didn't struggle because of what your mother did."

"When you put it like that, I can't deny it," he said, slumping back in the chair. The picture of Maxwell and Stanley mocked him from his computer screen. For the first few months he'd known Maxwell, Clayton thought the world of the man. He had nice clothes, and he always came bearing gifts. He paid the rent, gave them food, and then once he had gained their trust, he beat his mother into submission and held them both hostage.

Had Clayton known his mother spent three years stealing almost two million dollars from Maxwell, he might have played his cards differently as a young man, but it didn't matter anymore. His mom used most of the money for a good cause and left the rest to Clayton; only he hadn't touched a dime.

Where Sage grew up in a world where money solved problems, Clayton grew up in a world where money created issues.

"I care very much about all the people who come through the Alley Home." He focused on his pulse beating in his ears. It seemed to continue to increase, causing a tightness that he hadn't felt in a long time. He wasn't sure what it meant, but it brought an array of emotions he normally stifled without thinking about it.

"Everyone can tell you care, and you do so much, but it's obvious that you resent some of us who care differently." She heaved in a deep breath. "I know. I do the same thing; only it's masked in a smile while handing over a fat check to some other charity organization as I tell myself I'm better than my parents."

He waved his finger in the air. "We're different in that department. I never tell myself I'm better than my mother, because I know I'm not. I'm not better than anyone, but since I'm asking you to be honest with yourself, I should do the same."

"And what's your truth?"

"My mother was a decent woman. She didn't make the best choices in life, but she did the best she could with what she had, and I appreciate that. She's not the reason I come off as if the money that's given to the Alley Home isn't enough. I'm that way because of who my biological father is."

"I read somewhere that you have no idea who your father is."

"You shouldn't believe everything you read."

"I take it your mother told you who your father was?" Sage stood and cleared the table.

He took the laptop and moved to the sofa. Glancing over the top of the computer, he watched her move about the kitchen. She carried herself with more confidence than most young women he knew, but ever since he first struck up a conversation with her, he felt a kinship he didn't understand.

He hadn't even felt like that with his mother, who he had the utmost respect for, even if deep down he hadn't agreed with many of her life choices.

"She told me she had no idea, but I know that's a lie," he admitted for the first time out loud.

Sage tossed a dish rag over her shoulder and leaned against the kitchen sink. "Do you have a relationship with the man you think is your father?"

Now that was a loaded question and one he wasn't sure he wanted to answer truthfully. If Maxwell was indeed his biological father, then what did that mean for Clayton?

It would explain a lot of things in Clayton's life, specifically his inability to connect to a woman.

Or even have the desire to have a relationship.

But mostly, Clayton couldn't handle the fact that his father was a man who thought nothing of hitting a woman. Clayton believed that he could never, but after spending ten years in the military, he'd found out he was capable of taking human life.

Perhaps his father's genetics, if Maxwell was his dad, had rubbed off on Clayton in more ways than one. Something he never wanted to find out.

"We know each other."

"Is he in Vegas?"

Clayton shook his head. "I've never told anyone this before, and honestly, I'd rather drop the subject.

Besides, I have to read all these files that my boss sent over on your folks and their business."

"What am I supposed to do?" She tossed the towel on the counter. "I can't just sit around and do nothing."

Typically, he'd want to go over everything before discussing it with a client, but Sage made him want to toss any rule he might have had out the window. "I have an old tablet in the nightstand next to my bed. I'll open some of the documents on that, and you can help me go through all of it." He patted the couch.

"What if I find out things about my parents I don't want to know?" she asked, folding her arms across her chest.

"I think it's safe to say that's already happened." He dropped his head back and let the air in his lungs push through his nose. "I need to tell you something." His vocal cords rattled against his throat, causing a slight tremble to the sound of his voice. "The car that shot at us in the parking garage was owned by a holding company that your father owns."

"What? No way. You have to be joking." Her hands dropped to her sides, smacking against her legs. "That can't be possible."

"I wish it wasn't true. I'll understand if you no longer want to go through—"

She held up her hand. "Hell, no. I'm tired of hiding from the truth."

He cocked his head. "Then tell me what you're not telling me because I know you've left some things out."

She raised her hand and bit down on her nail. "Two things."

"Babe, if we're going to get to the bottom of this, you're going to have to tell me everything, no matter what."

"The real reason I don't want to ever set foot in the Alley Home is because it's your mother who was the prostitute my father was with." Her gaze darted around the room before landing on him and sucker, punching his gut.

He'd met many of his mother's johns, and it always made for an uncomfortable situation, but nothing in his past could have prepared him for those words coming from Sage's mouth.

"Are you sure about that?" he asked.

"When I was home for the holidays shortly before your mom died, I heard my parents arguing about her, and my mom said if he didn't call it off, she was going to ruin him."

"Most people bounce back from a sex scandal these days."

She shook her head. "No. She told my dad that she'd turn him in, making sure she came out smelling like a victim."

# CHAPTER 5

SAGE FLATTENED her hands across her stomach. "My parents are criminals. There is no denying that fact," she mumbled, passing the tablet back to Clayton. For the last twenty-four hours, they combed through all the materials Hank had sent over, and while it appeared her father only had surface dealings with Maxwell and other members of organized crime, there was still enough there for her to make that judgment call. She rubbed her sleep-deprived eyes. A few hours here and there wasn't enough rest, but she couldn't settle down. Clayton seemed to have the same problem. They took short breaks, walking through the campground, discussing music or anything that wasn't directly related to the case.

She'd learned more about him than she knew about her own parents.

"Technically, my mother was a criminal." Clayton's

words did nothing to ease the anger she had toward her parents.

And herself.

All these years she'd known. She'd seen things. She'd heard things, but never did she allow herself to believe what was right in front of her. But now that her mind was open, it all made perfect sense.

"We don't know exactly what your parents are involved in." He set his computer and the tablet on the coffee table. He patted his thighs. "Why don't you put your head down for a bit. You barely slept last night."

"Neither did you." She didn't fight him as she sprawled out on the sofa. Her muscles were tired. Her eyes burned. And her head ached.

He threaded his fingers through her hair, gently massaging her scalp.

Closing her eyes, she hugged his legs and let her body relax. "We know that three of the companies my father currently owns, Maxwell has a stake in the business. What I don't understand is why doesn't anyone know this? I mean, Maxwell is practically a household name. If my parents were involved with him illegally, I think everyone and their brother in Vegas would know about it."

"Not necessarily. Besides, it was Maxwell's LLC that had been an investor, so maybe your parents didn't know that until after because it took some digging for Hank to find all this out."

"So, what you're saying is it's possible my parents accidentally fell into a life of crime."

"I'm saying; we don't have enough facts to know the truth. And yes, that's possible. I've seen it before. Or maybe Maxwell had something on your father, and he's been blackmailing him. My boss sent a coworker of mine by the name of Dustin to act as a bodyguard for your parents."

"But he's there to gather information, right?"

"That would be part of it, but your father did admit to being threatened recently, so we want to take every necessary precaution."

"I'm shocked my father agreed to a bodyguard."

"He hasn't."

"Oh, he's not going to like Dustin just showing up then," she said.

"I suppose not, but we need to cover all our bases."

She rolled to her back and stared up at Clayton. "How do you feel about the fact that my father paid to be with your mother?"

"He's not the only man who's done that."

"It doesn't bother you?" Without thinking, she reached up and palmed his cheek.

"I was raised by a village of hookers. I saw a different side of that world than most people. While I don't agree with prostitution, I don't condemn those who partake, except for the assholes who feel the need to use their fists."

"It had to have been hard to grow up like that." All

73

her life, she never wanted for material things. But her life felt empty.

"No harder than being shipped off to boarding school and summer camp. You grew up feeling unloved and unwanted. I grew up knowing I was loved, but, if I'm honest, I felt unnoticed half the time. I believed I was the reason my mother ended up being a prostitute because she had to care for me, but the reality was she had started selling her body before I was born, and I know she never stopped, even when she opened the Alley Home."

"How did Maxwell find out about all the money your mom stole?"

"At first, he'd thought it was someone else and had that person killed. A few months later, he pinned it on another person. Three people died before my mother couldn't take it and told him that she'd stolen the money. He didn't handle that well, and a few weeks later, my mom was at the bottom of Lake Mead. I think there is more to that story, but whatever it is, it died with my mother, and Maxwell certainly isn't going to fill me in."

"I'm so sorry." She rose to a sitting position, cupping his face. "I can see in your eyes how much this hurt you, but you bottle it up too deep that I'm worried you've never really felt the loss."

"I've dealt with this," he said matter-of-factly. "I've seen a lot of death, and while it doesn't make it easier, it is part of life."

"Maybe you accept death and are at peace with your mother's, but it's the rest of the story that either you don't know, or don't want to verbalize that's holding your emotions hostage." She searched his face for any sign of the real guttural feelings he had to have about what happened to his mother, and the unanswered questions about her murder.

"I've made my peace with who my mother was, but you're right, Maxwell is a different story. He's a bad man."

"And my father is mixed up with him somehow."

"I'm afraid so, but we don't know if it has anything to do with you being kidnapped."

"I think I should tell you something." She tried to stand, but Clayton held her to his lap.

"Tell me what?"

Her pulse tickled her throat as it sped up. "I met Maxwell once."

"What?" Clayton cocked his head. "Why are you just now telling me this?"

"I didn't meet him as in had a conversation with him. When I first moved back to Vegas, I showed up at my parents' office unannounced and saw Maxwell having a heated discussion with both my parents. I honestly didn't think anything of it at the time."

"Seriously? A known gangster is hanging out with your family, and you shrug it off?"

She studied Clayton's face. The curve of his mouth. The dimple in his square jaw. And those Mediterranean blue eyes that tried to hide his kind soul and failed miserably. But it was the color and shape that gave her a shiver.

"I'm sorry. I shouldn't have gotten upset," he said, running his fingers through her hair, stopping to dance across the top of her shoulder. "Maxwell can be charming, and there are many upstanding citizens who do business with him, and he even had a senator fight for his casinos and clubs."

She nodded, appreciating his message and how he delivered it. But her curiosity got the better of her. "Who do you believe is your father?"

"You're a persistent woman," he said. "And smart. So, I think you've already figured out what I think." He closed his eyes and let out a long breath. "I asked my mother if Maxwell was my father when I was sixteen. She told me to never utter such insanities in front of anyone ever again. Considering the man used to beat the shit out of her, and he hit me a couple of times, I thought it best to heed her warning."

"Wow," she whispered right before pressing her mouth against his. She didn't feel pity for him, not at all, but she did empathize with the lost little boy who didn't like where he came from, and she suspected part of him didn't want to accept the truth, something she could relate to.

"What are you doing?" he asked, holding her cheeks between his strong hands.

"You wanted to kiss me earlier."

"I did, but why are you doing it now because—"

She kissed him hard, swirling her tongue around his, not letting him finish his statement. She straddled him, and his hands squeezed her hips. She hadn't had a lot of experience with men. Hell, she hadn't even lost her virginity until her twenty-first birthday, and that hadn't been an earth-shattering experience. The guy she'd been with had been kind and gentle, but not boyfriend material.

Most of the men she dated weren't cut out to be husbands, and she suspected she picked that type on purpose. Her idea of marriage had been stripped from her the day she found her father liked to pay for sex, and her mother had never left, even when she threatened to do so.

And if she were frank with herself, she'd seen her father with other women, and other not so up-and-up businesspeople, which was probably one of the reasons they sent her away. Maybe they told themselves it was to protect her, or maybe it was so they didn't have to deal with her, but that didn't matter anymore.

What mattered was that she was no longer going through life with blinders on.

Nope. Her eyes were wide open.

Clayton deepened the kiss while his hands roamed her body. His touch was as soft and gentle as a feather. His tongue masterfully found every crevice. He tasted like a combination of bitter coffee with a splash of creamy candy.

"I don't think I'm supposed to sleep with the clients," he whispered in her ear.

"Then, don't think."

He dropped his forehead to hers and held her face, his breathing labored. "You're so young."

"My age bothers you." She stiffened her spine. Two days ago, she played up the age difference, acting like a child because he kept reminding her that she might lack experience and maturity. But for him to point it out now was a bit of a buzzkill.

Not to mention insulting.

He ran his thumb over her bottom lip. "No. It doesn't. But you did call me an old man."

She opened her mouth, but he palmed her lips.

"I am fifteen years older, and I have nothing to offer you."

"What the hell does that mean?" Her heart hammered in her chest, pounding against her throat, making it hard to swallow, much less speak.

"While I've never been ashamed of where I came from, I am a slightly broken man. I have no desire for a lasting relationship. I don't want children. I never want to get married. I will live out the rest of my days in this trailer, knowing that at any time, I can move to another place if I want. I have no ties to anything except the Brotherhood Protectors, but even that is more about the job. I was put on this earth to protect and serve, and I love what I do, but that's about all the passion I have. Do you understand.?"

"I understand that you believe that, but if you could see what I do behind your stoic expressions, you'd see a man who cares so deeply he'd lay down his freedom for a complete stranger."

"As I said, that's all the passion I have, and this can't go any further if you can't accept that about me, because you and I will be nothing more than two ships passing in the night."

"I don't accept your lack of passion. But I do agree with everything else. For the record, I don't want marriage, kids, or any of that. My parents kind of destroyed any desire I might have had the day they told me I couldn't come home for Thanksgiving when I was twelve."

"That's cold."

"When all this is done before you head back to Montana, I have one request of you."

"Besides sex?" He winked.

She smiled as every erogenous zone in her body lit up like the Fourth of July. "I want you to show me around the Alley Home."

His jaw dropped open. "Are you serious?"

"Yes. You showed me the error of my ways, and I do want to make a difference with more than writing a check or raising money."

"I'd be honored."

"So, how about we take this to the bedroom," she said boldly. Her sexual experiences had left her wondering what the big deal had been. She'd gotten more satisfaction out of pleasuring herself than the act of making love. Of course, she had a few partners that had given her an orgasm, but they had been anticlimactic. She nearly laughed at her own pun.

It had never been the sex that had been disappointing, but what happened after while she lay there, naked, waiting until she could jump from the bed, get dressed, and take off running. She never knew what the proper amount of time for cuddling should be and because she didn't like to snuggle, being in a man's arms made her crazy.

The first few times she'd spent the night with a man, she ended up sneaking from the bed and snoozing on the sofa. Sharing her private space wasn't something she did well.

He lifted her into his arms and carried her the ten paces to the bedroom. Carefully, he laid her down. He stood at the edge of the bed and just stared at her.

Raised up on her elbows, she swallowed the fear that he might reject her. That quickly went away as he lifted his shirt and tossed it to the floor.

She jumped to her knees and ran her finger across the outline of the Navy SEAL insignia on his chest. She'd seen pictures of it but never tattooed on a man's pec before. Leaning in, she pressed her lips against his skin and inhaled sharply. Blinking, she noticed words tattooed on the left side of his torso. She glided her hand across his stomach, reading the words: *You've only got three choices in life: Give up, give in, or give it all you got.*

"Are these all the tattoos you have?"

Without saying a word, he turned, showing off a bald eagle spread across his shoulders and upper back. He rotated once more, and a small heart with the words: *Alley Home* written in the middle dotted his shoulder.

"That's sweet."

"My mom had the same one. We did it together one of the times I came to visit."

"Did you come home often?" She rested her hands on his shoulders, massaging gently, staring into his wondrous eyes. She found herself not only wanting to explore his body but his mind as well.

"I tried to visit at least once a year, but I was deployed the majority of the time I was in the service. Sometimes I think I did that to hide from some of the realities in Vegas that I didn't want to deal with."

"You're a good man, Clayton."

He took her hand and kissed her palm. "I wouldn't say that, but I am a man with a code."

She smiled. "That code is your way of hiding being so purely human that you have to be the most dangerous man I've ever met."

He cocked his head. "What does that mean?"

"If I were any other woman, I'd end up falling for you." She scooted back on the bed, rocking on her heels. In a quick swoop, she lifted her shirt over her head, exposing her bare breasts.

He groaned.

She loved the sound of the deep rumble that echoed through the room, giving her goosebumps.

"Do you have any tattoos?" He looped his fingers into the top of his jeans, snapping open the button at the top.

"I have two." She plopped to her butt and wiggled out of her shorts. She'd been eighteen when she had gotten her first tattoo on the small of her back. Her father had flipped when he saw it about a year later.

The next day, she'd gone out and gotten her second tattoo.

"Even the darkest night will end, and the sun will rise." He read the words on her back that had been etched inside a sunrise over a lake.

His fingers glided across her spine, hitting a ticklish spot, and she arched her back. "Where is the other one?"

She swallowed. She tried for the last few years to forget the day her father found her second tattoo. She'd been home visiting, lounging by the pool, reading a book when her father happened by.

The words that came out of his mouth, she'd pushed from her memory, but every once in a while, they tickled her mind.

She lay down on her back and spread her legs.

"Now that's an interesting tattoo."

She glanced down at the serpent slinking up her leg —the snake's head is hidden inside her panties.

"Is there a tongue that's reaching to a place I want to go to right now?"

"Why don't you find out for yourself." Thank God she was obsessive-compulsive about making sure she waxed regularly. Otherwise, the snake's head and tongue might be covered.

"That has to be the sexiest thing I've ever seen." His pink tongue popped out of his mouth, and he licked his way over the body of the snake, up to the inside of her thigh to…

"Oh, my God." She moaned as she dropped her head back to the pillow.

His hands continued to knead her legs and ass while his hot tongue brought her the kind of pleasure that she'd only imagined.

She dared to peek open her eyes and gasped when she locked gazes with him. His hands roamed up her body, cupping her breasts. His thumbs rolled across her tight nipples.

Her toes curled as she jerked and twisted, clamping his head between her legs. If it hadn't felt so good, she would be embarrassed about how quickly he'd been able to take her over the edge. Just when she thought she could relax, he slipped his fingers inside her and wiggled them in such a way that she raised her hips, grabbed her breasts, and cried out. "Clayton," she managed between ragged breaths.

She couldn't get enough oxygen to fill her lungs, but she didn't care. Her body had all that it needed, and it came in the form of a six-foot-three sexy protector with magic hands and an enchanting tongue. Her body shivered in anticipation of finding out how the rest of him filled her.

He kissed her stomach just above her belly button before kneeling between her legs.

She reached for the zipper of her pants.

He batted her hand away.

"Hey. No fair."

"Let's just say I forgot to put on my undergarments, and the pressure is a tad painful, so perhaps it's better if I do it."

"Is it a hurts so good kind of pain?" she asked boldly.

"You have no idea how good." He slipped from the bed and lowered his pants to the floor.

"Oh, my," she whispered as she bit down on her lower lip.

Every muscle in his body flexed. His tanned skin shined in the setting sun rays filtering through the window.

She took him into her hands. The sharp contrast between soft skin and solid mass warmed her body, giving her another shiver. She watched her hands glide up and down.

He let out a deep, guttural groan as she brought her lips to the tip of him. His hands fisted her hair, and she took him in slowly, trying not to gag, but she could only handle so much.

His touch remained tender, and he didn't push her as other men had in the past. She enjoyed assertive lovemaking, but she wasn't a fan of overly aggressive behavior. But what Clayton offered seemed to be the best of both worlds because she found herself being shamelessly immodest in her overt sexual acts. She stroked him faster and squeezed harder. She took as much of him in her mouth as she could, only to repeat the motion. When she glanced up at him, he stared at her with an admiring gaze. He let her do what she wanted, and he seemed to more than enjoy every second.

Gently, he tugged at her hair and then lifted her off the bed before laying her back down on her back. He rummaged through the nightstand until he found a condom.

She watched in awe as he covered himself in the protection. She held her breath as he eased between her legs. He raised his torso, planting his hands on either side of her head.

"You're are the most beautiful woman I've ever known."

It was impossible to contain her smile. "I'm sure you say that—"

He covered her lips with a quick kiss. "I mean it. I don't think there could ever be a woman as gorgeous as you. Inside and out."

Tears stung the corners of her eyes as she stared at a man who just showed her his soul. The world around her blurred. All that mattered was this moment in time.

The lines around his eyes softened. His warm lips kissed her neck, and he whispered sweet things in her ear. Things she wouldn't expect to come from a man who, at first glance, was far from a romantic.

Wrapping her arms and legs around his body, she lifted her hips in a desperate need to feel him release inside her. Never before had a man's pleasure meant so much to her. She rocked with him, following his lead, hoping she did exactly what he wanted, needed.

He fanned his hands over her cheeks. "You've changed me."

She gasped as he took her mouth in a hot, wet, sloppy kiss. Their bodies molded together like the stars blanketed the night sky. A wave of dizziness overtook her as he slammed inside her over and over again until her body shook in a violent surge that left her breathless.

Arching his back, he groaned, holding his body steady for a long moment before he gently lowered himself on top of her, rolling his hips in slow motion.

She ran her hands up and down his back, her legs still tightly wrapped around his ass. For the first time in her life, she wanted to hold this man, all night, and never let go.

## CHAPTER 6

*DING.*

*Ding.*

Clayton blinked his eyes open, surprised that both his arms were still wrapped around Sage's body. He'd never been one to be able to sleep with another human in his bed, so he usually didn't. But everything about Sage was different.

He picked up his cell and stared at a text from Dustin.

*DUSTIN: Stanley Adams is acting squirrely. He doesn't want me here and thinks it's a waste of resources. He keeps taking phone calls, excusing himself to the other room and whispering. He's not very cooperative, and I know he's not truthful. I think he knows who tried to kidnap Sage, but he won't admit it, and now he's demanding to see her, so I'm bringing him over, now. Hank said it was okay.*

Shit.

Clayton glanced at sleeping beauty. It would take Dustin a good half hour or so to get to the campground, so he'd let her sleep a little while longer. He knew her father would bring out the worst in her, and Clayton didn't want to upset her before he had to.

She had suffered enough at the hands of her parents. Sadly, more was to come, but Clayton would do his best to protect her.

He'd grown up in a home where falling in love wasn't an option. Hell, his mother didn't believe in love or marriage. To her, all those things did was to bring about heartache and pain. Of course, when pressed, his mother swore she'd never been in love.

Except he saw how she looked at Maxwell. How she always let him in and out of her life. She once told Clayton that she did so just because of the money she'd been stealing, but he knew better. He also knew that one week before his mother had been murdered, she'd been with Maxwell again. He was one of the reasons Clayton rarely came back to Vegas. Guilt still plagued him. He should have protected his mother better, even though she was a fiercely independent woman.

He slipped from the bed and Sage's arms. Hiking up his jeans, he padded toward the kitchen. It was close to six in the morning, and the sun had already started to lighten the sky. Not surprising he was awake, but it was shocking he'd slept through the night, something he didn't ever remember doing. He snagged a glass of orange juice and fired up his laptop.

"Hey, Siri, call Dustin," he said into his phone.

It went straight to voicemail.

Clayton wouldn't mind spending a few hours with Mr. and Mrs. Adams if only to give them a piece of his mind for not caring for their daughter as they should have. She'd probably come out a better person for having been on her own for so long.

Her large bank account concerned him almost as much as how she'd turned his world upside down. He'd never met a woman quite like Sage. She was a unique blend of confidence, intelligence, with a tiny splash of innocence. She was willing to learn and change, but mostly, she'd changed him on one very fundamental level.

She opened the dam, and he didn't think he'd ever be able to go back to the removed man he was before she sashayed into his world.

His buddy Kick, who'd just gotten married and had a kid on the way, told him that when love happens, there isn't a damn thing you can do to stop. But that didn't mean Clayton had to take to it like a fish in a fresh tank. Somehow he'd have to shake this sudden desire to buy a house and settle down somewhere.

He scanned the few emails he'd gotten that highlighted Stanley's career. On the outside, he looked like a self-made millionaire, but as Clayton's team dug deeper, it appeared Stanley had a little help from organized crime.

The lead Stanley Adams had given them about Rotork hadn't panned out. Sure, the family had been bitter about the takeover, and they'd been vocal, selling their story to the tabloids, but nothing in the team's research indicated the Rotork family had gone rogue.

The best thing that could happen would be finding either Nolan or the man that drove the car in the parking garage. Of course, that could have been Nolan as well. He wasn't the kind of man who gave up. No. Nolan liked a challenge, and as long as someone had paid him, he'd do the honorable thing among criminals...and finish the job.

That was unless someone paid him to skip out on the job.

Clayton let out a long breath and made himself a cup of coffee. He sipped the tar-flavored water and stared in the direction of the bedroom. He'd had one attempt at a relationship, and it made him crazy. Everything in his life had become a chore, and he'd been miserable. He didn't like answering to anyone, except maybe Hank, but that was different. The Brotherhood Protectors were a unique blend of a particular type of men and women who had no problem putting human life in front of their own.

But even many of those men and women managed

to find love. He remembered the first time he'd met Hank's wife. She'd been kind and sweet, but she had a certain edge to her that all the women of the Brotherhood had. Clayton knew it took a specific personality type to live with and love a military man, and it was not different for the Brotherhood.

But Clayton didn't want a family, much less a wife. It honestly hadn't been anything he'd ever really thought about.

Until he'd climbed into bed with Sage Adams.

A surge of jealousy slithered through his veins for any other man who had been in her life or any future man that might come after him.

Mind-blowing sex.

That's all it was. She had been the best he'd ever had. Someone had to have that title and for him, the best he'd ever had happened to be Sage.

Headlights outside his trailer, caught his attention. Quickly, he found his weapon and carefully opened the front door.

"Dustin," Clayton said as he pulled back the door. He frowned the second he laid eyes on Stanley Adams, even though he knew they were on the way.

"Where's my daughter?" Stanley barked without saying hello. Not even a firm handshake.

Jerk.

Clayton became painfully aware that he stood in the doorway of the bedroom in only a pair of jeans, which weren't even fastened.

Worse, there wasn't a door into the other room, and if he glanced over his shoulder, he would get an eyeful of one sexy leg peeking out of his sheets.

"She's still asleep. It's been a long couple of days for her," Clayton said as matter-of-factly as he could muster, and that just pissed him right the fuck off. Never in his life had he been unable to remove emotion from his voice. He could handle the fierce protectiveness he felt, but the rest of it just clouded his judgment. "Why are you here?" Clayton kept his attention focused on Dustin for the time being.

"I'm the one paying both your salaries, and I wanted to see my daughter." Stanley had a defensive tone to his voice. "I want to make sure you're doing everything possible to keep her safe."

Dustin drew his lips into a tight line. He was one of the youngest men employed by the Brotherhood Protectors at the age of twenty-eight. He'd just re-enlisted in the Army when he'd been mortally wounded and ended up being medically discharged with another coworker, Shamus. Dustin was a good man, and he was good at his job, so Clayton had to believe he had a good reason for breaking protocol.

"Daddy?" Sage emerged from the bedroom, wearing only Clayton's shirt.

Clayton blushed, something he seldom did, and it appeared that hadn't gone unnoticed by Dustin, who smirked.

"What are you doing here?" Sage slipped her arm

around Clayton's middle, resting her head on his shoulder. Her fingernails sizzled his skin.

For the sake of his job, he should push her away, but he couldn't. He would give her whatever she wanted or needed, especially when it came to her parents. He wasn't entirely sure what to make of all the information regarding her father and his business, but thus far, none of it looked as if it were on the up-and-up.

"I was worried about you," her father said.

"You could have just called." Her voice was tight with thick emotion. The anger skimming across her body, coated his muscles. He'd gladly soak up any negative feeling she had. He'd do whatever it took to keep her safe.

And make her happy.

"I'd like a moment alone with my daughter," her father said.

Clayton turned to Sage, resting his hands on her hips and ignoring the palpable tension that filled the room. "You going to be okay?"

"Who the hell do you think you are?" Stanley took two steps forward.

Clayton held his hand out but didn't glance in his direction. "I'm the man who saved your daughter's life." He heaved in a heavy breath. "Dustin and I are going to step out. There is a fresh pot of coffee on the counter." Taking her chin between his thumb and forefinger, he kissed her lips gently. "I'll be right outside."

"How dare—"

Sage stepped between Clayton and her father.

Clayton puffed out his chest. He knew he'd catch shit from his boss about his idiotic behavior, but her father sent a shiver up his spine and not just because of the way Sage described how he treated her as a child.

"Daddy. Let's get you a cup of coffee." She pressed her hand on Clayton's back and gave him a slight shove toward the door with a narrowed stare.

Well, that didn't go well.

"What the hell are you doing?" Dustin asked the second the door slammed shut.

The desert sun rose over the mountains, warming the fresh air. In less than an hour, it would be twenty degrees warmer than it had been all night. Clayton turned and stared at the window into his trailer. At least the curtains remained open, and he could see inside.

"I don't give a shit that you slept with her, but pushing her father's buttons, that's just not a good idea, especially when I think he's the mastermind behind this entire thing," Dustin said in a low voice.

"If that's true, bringing him here was a huge mistake." Clayton swallowed his anger and did his best to suppress the unwelcome sensation that tingled throughout his entire system. Caring about someone on more than a surface level wasn't something he understood. Protecting someone was easy.

Protecting someone you loved complicated things,

and his thinking had already been altered. He inhaled sharply and focused on the situation at hand.

"We weren't followed," Dustin said. "And I made him turn off his phone and leave it in my glove box."

"Did you tell him where Sage and I were before you left his place?"

"Nope," Dustin said. He leaned against the trailer and chewed on a toothpick—annoying habit. But then again, Dustin could be annoying. He was young, arrogant, and still resented having to leave the Army for medical reasons.

He was good at what he did, but Clayton often wondered if Dustin had a death wish. He was undoubtedly an adrenaline junkie, always skydiving, bungee jumping, and racing cars—anything to keep his heart pumping at a dangerously high rate.

Another thing Clayton couldn't relate to. He didn't chase trouble because he got high off it. No. He chased danger because someone had to protect and serve, and he had the mindset.

"Trisha is working on hacking into his phone and home computer system, another reason Hank thought it was a good idea for me to bring Stanley here." Dustin popped the toothpick from his mouth before inserting it on the other side.

"Why do you think her father is behind this?" Clayton had to be missing some information because while he suspected Stanley to have dirty hands, there was nothing to suspect he'd want to hurt his own kid.

"Look at this." Dustin handed Clayton a cell phone.

Clayton sat down on the log in front of the firepit and stared at an image of Nolan sitting at a poker table with Maxwell, Stanley, and four other men Clayton knew to be involved in criminal activity. "When was this taken?"

"I have no idea. The picture is on a bookshelf in Stanley's office. When I first arrived, he was in the shower, so his wife told me to make myself at home, so I wandered. He wasn't too thrilled to see me in his office, and when he thought I wasn't looking, he took the picture and put it face down on his desk. Five minutes later, he's demanding to see his daughter."

"That doesn't make him the puppet master."

"That's not the only thing I'm basing my observation on."

Clayton handed Dustin his phone back. "I'm listening."

"I stepped outside to call Hank about Stanley's demands, and you know me, I have to pace when I talk on the phone. I did so up and down the side of the house. But instead of going back in the same way I came, I opted for the kitchen sliders, and I overheard Sage's parents talking. I didn't get the entire conversation, but Lorna Adams said something to the effect of *He's in prison, and we don't work for him anymore, so take care of it. I don't care what you have to do, including killing her, if that keeps our operations running.*" Dustin held up his hand.

"Stanley then told his wife that the plan was already in play. His wife then muttered off a couple of obscenities, the final one telling her husband if he could keep his dick in his pants, none of this would have happened."

Clayton rubbed the two-day-old scruff that had grown on his neck and face. "That still doesn't give us any reason to believe Stanley would try to kidnap his own daughter. What's his motivation, and how does Sage fit into all this?"

"She's collateral damage." Dustin sat on the tree trunk. "And you're the icing on the cake for taking him down and putting him behind bars."

"Kick and his wife and her family did that, not me." Clayton pinched the bridge of his nose. "But Maxwell did promise that he wouldn't rest until I was either behind bars or with my mother in hell."

"Everyone knew you'd be at that charity event. Maxwell must have something huge on Stanley and used it to get him to hire Nolan to kidnap her—"

"And there goes your theory," Clayton said. "Because I'm the one who foiled that plan."

"You did, but that doesn't mean you didn't play into Maxwell's hand." Dustin stretched out his legs, crossing one ankle over the other. "Maxwell's plans have always had layers and built-in go-to-shit plans. But once you became her protector, it opened the playing field for him to set you up as a murderer."

"That's pretty, far-fetched." Clayton's heart

thumped in an uneven rhythm against his throat. He couldn't swallow, and his mouth went dry.

Sadly, that made more sense than Clayton cared to admit.

"I bet Nolan knew you were following him, and everyone saw you leave right after the girls. The valet said he overheard you talking about going out with Sage, so if they disappeared, people might put that together. But where it gets ingenious is the backup layer."

The gears inside Clayton's head began to spin. "I take it Stanley started with wanting to talk with Sage."

"Exactly. But when the phone kept going to voice-mail, he checked the Find My iPhone app and got nothing, so he started demanding to know where she was and that I had to take him to her immediately."

"Shit. Where's his wife?" Clayton snapped his gaze to Dustin.

"She had some meeting at work. Maddog is watching her, though she doesn't know that. Trisha is working on hacking into their system, and she'll let us know when she's in."

"And what about Weslynn?"

"Frost has eyes on her," Dustin said.

"I don't like that. Too many chances of something bad happening to any one of them."

"I know. But I didn't see any other way under the circumstances. My guess is that as soon as I get Stanley out of here, he's going to need to make an important business call. Then it's only a matter of time before Nolan, or some other contract killer, ends up here, and you're both dead, or you, my friend, just became a murderer."

"I wish I had killed Maxwell when I had the chance," Clayton mumbled. What Dustin said all rang true, even if a shit-ton of it was conjecture. "But if you're wrong, then we're back to square one."

Dustin nodded. "We have two choices. We hang tight and set up a sting as best we can, or we move you, and I sit up here watching to see if anyone shows up, and then we make a plan going forward."

"I'm not moving. If he's sending someone after me, I'll be ready."

"We'll be ready. Hank sent Swede and Boomer. I'm just bummed I'm stuck babysitting the parents."

"When will Swede and Boomer get here?" Clayton trusted every man and woman in the Brotherhood Protectors, but working side by side with men he served with as SEALs gave him a much-needed sense of calm.

"They are in the bird on the way. We've rented the campsite next door." Dustin pointed to an empty parking spot just across the dirt road.

Clayton glanced over his shoulder. His trailer sat between the road and the lake, but he still didn't like the setup. Too many places a bad guy could penetrate the perimeter. "What are your parents like?"

"Excuse me?" Dustin opened his mouth, and his toothpick dropped to the ground.

"Are they overprotective? Too caring? Not caring enough? How did they fuck up your life?"

"That's a really fucking odd question."

"You know my adolescence wasn't much of a child-hood, so I'm trying to get a handle on the more normal dysfunction, and maybe then we can understand why the hell Stanley would do this to his daughter."

"I don't think their family is the typical normal dysfunctional unit you're talking about."

"Just humor me," Clayton said.

"My parents are awesome. They've always been supportive of me, even when they hate what I'm doing. My dad was pretty strict, but not unreasonable, and my mom now cries every time she sees me, but that's just because she can't get it out of her head what I looked like in the hospital after I nearly got blown up."

"I imagine that was tough for her. Do you think you are the man you are today because of how your parents raised you, or do you think it's just who you are? That genetics count more for how a person ends up than their environment."

Dustin narrowed his stare. "Is this about your father?"

"I don't have a father," Clayton said. "I have a sperm donor."

Dustin stood and stretched. "I think we end up a certain way based on a combination of genetics, our family, and our experiences in life and how they affect us." Dustin tapped his chest. "We've all suspected Maxwell was your father after the shakedown a few months ago. But just because Maxwell is a ruthless criminal, that doesn't make you one. Just like Sage isn't a mirror image of her parents, who by the way are the most uncaring people on the planet. They have a handful of pictures of Sage around the house, but when you ask questions about their daughter's life, they haven't a clue. Kind of sad if you ask me."

But Sage was more like her parents than Clayton cared to admit. Of course, writing checks to help out the less fortunate wasn't a bad thing at all, and Sage had said she wanted to do more, and he planned on holding her to that.

"We need to find out why Stanley is doing this, and instead of playing sitting ducks, we're going to find out right now." Clayton rose and took two steps toward the trailer before glancing over his shoulder. "Are you coming?"

"Oh, hell, yes," Dustin said.

Hopefully, when all was said and done, Sage wouldn't hate him for the nasty things he was about to say.

SAGE WATCHED Clayton walk out the front door, leaving her alone with her father.

When she'd woken up in bed by herself, she worried that maybe Clayton had regretted their night together, but then she'd heard her father's voice, and her stomach turned to cement. It was in that moment she knew without a doubt that it was time to stop lying to herself.

"Has that man hurt you?" her father asked, his tone filled with anger and maybe a hint of fear, not concern.

Sage had waited a lifetime for her parents to genuinely care about her well-being, but this wasn't the moment, and now she knew it would never come.

"Clayton wouldn't hurt anyone," she said firmly. "Why are you here, Dad?" She poured two cups of coffee and set one on the counter while she held the other one to her lips, trying not to gag on the horrible taste.

"Why aren't you answering your phone?" her father asked, leaning against the counter with his arms folded across his massive chest. His face contorted much like it had the day she made her last loan payment, something he used to try to control her with, but she was done with allowing anyone to control her actions. For years, she'd tried to please her parents without compromising herself, yet she failed miserably, on both accounts.

Only, standing in the middle of a mobile home, she realized there was no pleasing her parents. She could have done exactly what they asked of her, and she'd still feel as though she was nothing but a minor blip on their radar.

She had to wonder why they hadn't aborted her or given her up for adoption because the only thing she represented to them was a family photo opportunity so the media would focus on how great her father was, not that he crushed companies and the people who own them for sport.

"Clayton told me to keep it off until they caught whoever tried to kidnap me," she said, swallowing the bile that smacked the back of her throat.

"Is that *his* shirt you're wearing?" her father asked with a fair amount of disgust dripping from his tongue.

"It is," she admitted.

"God damn it. I'm going to give that man a piece of my mind for taking advantage of—"

"Stop blustering," she said as calmly as she could. "You don't give a shit about me or who I sleep with as long as it doesn't interfere with your work."

Her father gasped as if in shock. Maybe he was considering she'd seldom dared to talk back or be assertive. "I've been worried sick and now to think this dirty old man—"

"Clayton is a good man. I'm wearing his shirt because all I have is my red cocktail dress. The policeman who was supposed to bring me some clothes had something important to take care of and couldn't make it out here the last few days." She shouldn't have had to explain herself, but she didn't want her father to go off and hit Clayton, because that would only end badly for dear old dad.

"And what cop is that?"

Her pulse increased as hot blood raced through her veins, fueling the fire that burned in the pit of her stomach. Her father hadn't come here to check on her; he came to dig for information. The need for his approval died at that moment.

"I don't remember his name," Sage lied. Her gaze locked with her father's as she searched his eyes for a sign of…of…love, but she knew she'd never get it.

"Well, find out and then text me. I know people in high places, and I'm not satisfied with how this band of misfits is working out."

She wanted to ask him why it mattered but thought better of it. "You still haven't answered my question. Why did you come all the way out here? Because it wasn't out of concern for me."

"What has gotten into you? What has that man done to you?"

"You knew I was just fine, so come on, Dad. Tell me why you're really here?" Two days ago, Sage might have still been lying to herself about what she'd seen as a child in hopes of having some beautiful home life. But Clayton had changed all that by helping her to open her eyes. "Tell me why you didn't come to the charity event because you made a big deal about being there, but you never showed. Not a single phone call or text. Nothing. Why, Daddy?"

"I had to deal with a situation regarding one of my companies; otherwise, I would have been there. I heard it went well."

"Went, well? That's all you have to say? No pats on the back? No praise for a job well done? No apology for not coming?"

"Where is this coming from because, for your entire life, you've been fiercely independent, not needing a single thing from your mother or me."

She rolled her eyes. "Because I had no choice," she mumbled. "Why didn't Mom come?"

"Because, as my lawyer, I needed her."

Since she opened this line of questioning, she might as well put all her cards on the table. "Are you sure you didn't want to be there because you knew something bad was going to happen to me, and you didn't want to get caught in the crossfire?" Sage had been back in Vegas for three years, and she could count on one hand how often she had spent any time with her parents. Granted, she had been working eighty hours a week getting her foundation off the ground, but she still tried to carve out time for her parents. "Or maybe it's because you didn't want to be near the son of the woman you used to fuck."

"You have no idea what you're talking about," her father said.

"Interesting that you do not deny it."

"What kind of lies is this man filling your head

with? I hired him to protect you, not turn you against me with this insanity that you're spewing."

She laughed. "You must not think very highly of me if you believe one man could influence me so much." Only, Clayton had done precisely that. Or maybe she'd been slowly seeing the truth. Either way, she drew her own conclusions. "I'm tired of trying to get you to see me. To hear me. To support my life decisions. But, like last night, you couldn't be bothered. I think you want me to fall on my face."

"You believe your mother and I wanted you to fail? You've been running successful events for over a year now. Just because I think you're wasting your time and talents, doesn't mean I don't want the best for you."

"And what if I asked to come work for you? What would you say to that?"

"You have no desire to work for me or your mother. Not even when you were a little girl. All you ever talked about was living in Europe and—"

"You put all those thoughts in my head. I was told my entire life that I wasn't cut out for your line of work. Why?" Not that she wanted to tear companies apart, but she wanted her father to admit he didn't love her.

And neither had her mother.

"Because you had other interests and I wanted you to chase after them," her father said. He still had made no attempt to hug her or give her any kind of physical attention.

"And yet you discouraged me from every career I thought I might want to have. You told me to go find a rich husband or take up painting." She thought she understood last night why volunteering at places like the Alley Home was just as important as the money. Her father had given her every material thing she could ever want or need, but it didn't make up for the lack of affection in her life. If her father had rested his hand on her shoulder, kissed her cheek, given her even the smallest of embraces, that might have been enough to show her what being a human really meant.

"You're an ungrateful brat, and I have a feeling that man out there has charmed not only his way into your bed, but your brain as well."

She sucked in a deep breath, keeping the tears at bay. She wouldn't give her father the satisfaction. "My assistant was shot while some hitman tried to kidnap me, and you're standing over there more upset that I might have gone to bed with my protector."

"Have you? Because that would be a mistake. He's not a good man."

"And you know this how?" Her stomach churned sour as her father focused on everything but her.

"I know to which the world he was born," her father said.

"That's right, you often paid for sex with his mom, and I'm sure other hookers as well."

"Watch your mouth, young lady. You don't know

what the hell you're talking about, except for the fact that man out there is a bastard."

"He's more of a man than you are," Sage said under her breath.

Her father inched forward. "Not only is he the son of a prostitute, but his father is currently in jail."

"How would you know that?"

"I know things," her father said behind gritted teeth.

"If Clayton is such a horrible man, then why are you trusting him to protect me?"

"I didn't hire him, your mother did. If it were solely up to me, I'd have that foul man put down. But when your mother hears what's going on here, she'll fire him, and we'll get someone else."

The front door creaked open. Clayton stepped into the family room with an arched brow and his arms folded across his bare chest.

"Go ahead and fire him." She pointed at Clayton. "As a matter of fact, I insist."

Her father turned his head and smiled. "All right. Both of you, your services are no longer needed. My daughter and I will be leaving."

"You will be leaving, but I'm staying right here," Sage said as she waltzed across the room and wrapped her arms around Clayton. She glanced up at him, then rested her hand on the center of his chest. "Clayton will take care of me whether he's been hired to or not."

"Sage, darling. You don't know what the hell you're doing." Her father stomped across the room.

Clayton shoved her behind his back.

"I have no idea what just happened here, but I'm not leaving her side until I know she's safe. Dustin can take you back to your house. If you don't want him to protect you and your wife, call my boss, and Dustin will be gone, but Sage is staying with me."

"Over my dead body," her father said with clenched fists. His eyes were wide with rage.

"I'm not leaving, Daddy."

"You're going to pay for this," her father jabbed Clayton in the arm with his index finger. "I can't make her come with me, but I will make sure you're finished in this Brotherhood thing."

"Good luck with that," Clayton said.

"I demand you take me home." Her father breezed past them, the door slamming shut behind him.

"Get him out of here and call me later," Clayton said.

Dustin nodded and left.

Clayton turned and glared. "What the hell happened in here?"

"I realized my father isn't a very good man." She brushed her hair from her face. "He didn't come here to see if I was okay, he came here to fish for information, and when he didn't get what he wanted, he pushed it all back on me and well…on you too."

"Put it on me? How?"

Her lashes fluttered over her eyes as she tried to divert his gaze. "He's confident Maxwell is your father, and he thinks somehow you're the bad guy in this."

Clayton's eyebrows shot up. "Other than to my coworkers and you, I've never uttered those words, so I have no idea how he's come to that conclusion. But what's more disturbing is that he walked out of here without you."

She rubbed the side of her neck. "I'm accepting my parents are total strangers to me, but my father is a control freak. If he's not in charge of his surroundings, he finds a way to flip that in his favor. He doesn't sit in the passenger seat, ever."

"Are you talking literally?"

She nodded. "He either drives, or has his diver take him, or he gets a limo. So, letting Dustin drive him out here doesn't make sense."

"It's starting to pull together for me," Clayton said.

"How so?"

"He needed to know where you were, and we weren't about to give him the address because Dustin thinks your dad is behind your kidnapping, and I'm starting to agree with Dustin."

Her heart dropped to her gut. "I'm no longer surprised."

# CHAPTER 7

"I'M SORRY ABOUT YOUR FOLKS."

Sage rested her head on Clayton's chest, enjoying his fingers gliding through her hair as he held her close. She felt horrible about how she'd first treated him, but she'd done so out of fear and anger. When Clayton had contacted her about the fundraiser, she almost said no, but something in the back of her mind told her this event would be the one that put her on the map.

"None of this is your fault," she said, tilting her head. "Is this really your home?"

He nodded.

"Ever live with anyone in here?"

He shook his head. "I have a difficult time sharing space with anyone."

"Well, that makes sense. This place is tiny."

"I could be in a mansion, and I wouldn't want to live with anyone."

Pressing her lips against the center of his chest, she inhaled his musky scent. "Do you want to hear something crazy?"

"Sure."

"Last night was the first night I stayed all night in the same bed with a man. Normally, I sneak out in the middle of the night because it feels vulnerable to sleep next to someone."

He lifted her chin and stared deeply into her eyes. "I'm a loner. Have been my entire life and even I don't have a problem doing that. But I don't stay for breakfast, and I make sure they leave first thing. The morning after is often awkward."

"This wasn't awkward. Well, except for my dad showing up." Butterflies filled her stomach, and a warmth spread over her skin like hot fudge on ice cream.

He dropped his forehead to hers and let out a short breath. "Don't ever think badly of yourself because of your father."

"Easier said than done."

"You're a good woman," he whispered.

"I mistreated you from the second we met. I'm sorry about that."

"I judged you pretty harshly as well."

"You only thought I was younger than I am," she

said. "And I'm well aware I look more like I'm in my late teens than my mid-twenties."

"Well, I all but called you incompetent."

"That is true." She looped her arms around his shoulders. "But I wanted nothing to do with you based on who your mother was. That's cold."

"I get that a lot."

"It's not fair." She raised on tiptoe and pressed her lips against his neck just under his earlobe. "Tell me something."

"Tell you what?" He bent over and curled his fingers around her thighs, then hoisted her off the ground.

She wrapped her legs around his waist. "Why don't you want a family?"

His right brow arched. "I'll answer that, but you've also stated that marriage and kids are out of the question, so I want to know why."

"Age before beauty."

He groaned as he laid her down on the bed. His fingers fumbled with the buttons on her shirt. "I don't think I'd make for a good father."

"Why not?" She batted his hands away. "You're so kind and caring."

He let out a chuckle. "You've never seen me around kids. They terrify me."

She fanned her thumbs across his cheekbones. "I bet you turn to mush around kids. So, tell me the real reason."

He flopped onto his back, resting his head on his

hand. "You're right. I do go gaga over children, but I'm not cut out to raise them. I get too restless and need the freedom to be able to get up and go anytime I want."

"How long were you a Navy SEAL?"

"About ten years."

"That takes commitment and drive." She found herself wanting to know about all the things he shoved into a dark corner somewhere in his mind. He did his best to hide his true self, but she knew once she peeled the layers back, the real Porter Clayton would shine through.

"But it changes all the time. Different places. Different ops. Every day is different. It's the same old same old that gets to me."

She thrived on routine and procedure, but she certainly understood his point. A little excitement was a good thing. "And how long have you lived in Montana working for the Brotherhood Protectors?" She rolled to her side and propped her head up on her hand. No man had ever made her feel as though she could be herself, especially when lying in bed half naked, but Clayton made her want to get real about everything in her life.

"Ten years."

"What do you do when you don't have an assignment?" When she'd been in college, one of her professors told her that the key to getting someone to invest in anything was to spend a few moments asking probing questions. The narrative that Clayton followed didn't allow him to invest in himself fully. He hid behind his talents and his honor much like she hid from facing the fact that it wasn't his mother, or women like her, that upset Sage.

It was men like her father, and if she didn't go to the shelters and educational facilities, then she wouldn't have to admit her father wasn't a very good man.

And her mother wasn't much better.

"My buddy Taz's wife is a physical therapist. She has a ranch close by and does a lot of work with veterans who were injured. I help her out wherever I can."

"Do you hear yourself? You have the sweetest, kindest heart of any man I've ever met."

"I have my moments," he said with a smile.

"You might think you're a nomad, but you gave these wheels roots. What else do you think is keeping you from falling in love and having kids?"

"Every job I've ever had is dangerous and takes me away, like right now, often for days or weeks. I'm not giving that up, and that's not fair of a wife or kid to have me gone all the time." He ran his hand up and down his bare chest while staring at the ceiling. "What about you? What are your reasons?"

He looked relaxed, but there was a somber look to his face. She understood his position, and she felt the same way. Why bring a kid into this world when you know you're going to be too busy to spend any time raising them.

"I'm afraid that I'm more like my parents than I care to admit." She rested her chin on his biceps. Growing up, she had very few close friends. She spent her time thinking of ways to make her parents proud. To make them want to spend time with her. She'd done everything from trying to get expelled to receiving straight As. "I'm afraid that I will look at my husband and be bored and then cheat on him. I've already done that once."

"You've been married?" he asked with a playful smile.

She laughed. "God, no. But I was in a serious relationship while in college, and I found his roommate a little more exciting."

"Ouch."

"I know. I felt so guilty. I didn't love him, but he didn't deserve what I did to him."

Clayton reached out and brushed her hair from her face. "So, you believe you're destined to be a cheater and not love your child."

"Something like that," she said.

"You're young. You have plenty of time to chase your dreams and have a husband you adore and a child to love if you want."

"Have you chased your dreams?"

"I'm not sure I have dreams," he said. "I once watched Maxwell hit my mother."

She opened her mouth, but he hushed her with a short, but powerful kiss.

"I was so scared, but I wanted to protect my mother, so I tried to stop him." Clayton rolled to his side and rested his hand over the words tattooed on his body. "I covered up the scars that he created when he took a knife to my side to teach me a lesson."

"Clayton, I'm so sorry."

His thumb traced her lower lip. "When we took Maxwell down a few months ago, he told me he knew he was my father. That my mother had done a paternity test but never shared with me the results."

"Do you believe him?"

Clayton nodded. "Not at first, but I saw the results when I cleaned out my mother's house after she died. While I know that fundamentally, I'm a good person, I know all too well that even the best people can do horrible things."

"I can't imagine you've done anything horrible."

"I've killed people."

"In combat?" she asked.

He nodded. "That doesn't change the fact I'm capable of taking a life. My mother was a whore, and she never stopped. My father is a gangster, and even from behind bars, he's tugging at my strings. Not only am I a damaged man, but my genetics suck. I wouldn't want to pass that on to any child."

Tears stung her eyes like sandpaper. Listening to his reasoning made her realize that she'd used her parents as an excuse to be less than a whole woman. She wasn't just the product of her parents' genetics. No. She was so much more, and she deserved to dream. She deserved to go after anything and everything.

And so did he.

"I know you'd make for a great husband and an even better father."

"Well, it's never going to happen. But for the record, you will be the best mother ever, and any man who didn't appreciate the kind of woman you are as well as understanding your needs is a total moron." He slipped his tongue between her lips and rolled over on top of her. His touch was tender and needy, but not desperate. He kissed her mouth, her neck, and her collarbone. His hands roamed across her body, carefully removing the rest of her clothes, leaving her naked on the bed.

"You take my breath away," he said as he ran his fingers up her arm, across her chest, and down her stomach. "You make me want to re-think my entire life."

Her lashes fluttered, and her vision blurred. With every deep breath, her lungs burned.

He removed his clothing and settled between her legs, entering her slowly.

"I have a confession to make," he whispered in her ear.

"You want to do that right now?"

She locked her legs around his waist and raised her hips.

A deep, throaty growl filled the room.

"I had no intention of coming to the fundraising

event until I saw an interview that a local news show had done on you, and I had to come to meet you."

Deliberately and leisurely, he rolled his hips, gently stroking her insides.

"You don't need to flatter me; we're already in bed and already—"

"Whenever an event like this happens, I usually just cut the ribbon or show up at the shelter to volunteer. I don't put on a suit and go to dinner with people I have nothing in common with. But I wanted to know you. I went out of my way to be in the same room with you."

Her chest rose and fell as she struggled to catch her breath. She dug her heels into the mattress and gripped his shoulders. She feared she might pass out from the pure pleasure he gave her body. It made her brain fuzzy as if she'd been drinking mimosas for breakfast.

His gaze held her captive. She couldn't turn away even if she wanted to. A slight tremble started in her toes and continued up her legs to her core. A warm shiver glided across her skin. Orgasms had never come easy to her during sex. She had to concentrate so intently to get close, but either it faded into the background or stopped altogether, leaving her utterly unsatisfied.

Something told her that Clayton never disappointed anyone.

He bent over and took one of her nipples into his mouth. He scraped the sensitive nub with his teeth.

She hissed and arched her back, pushing harder

against his hips. Desperation took over her mind and soul. Wiggling underneath his weight, she closed her eyes and increased the friction between their bodies.

"Look at me," he commanded.

She blinked her eyes open and gasped. Reaching up, she cupped his face. Soft moans filled the room like music trickling from an overhead speaker. It was quiet and subtle but so powerful. The sound sent her over the edge. A crushing sensation gripped her heart. Her pulse raced in her ears. She flexed her toes and prepared herself for the onslaught of the unknown. Tossing her head back and forth, she moaned. "Clayton," she whispered.

Effortlessly, he lifted her from the bed.

"What are you doing?"

"I want you to see what I see." He set her down in front of the dresser and turned her toward the mirror.

She swallowed, hard, while she stared at her reflection. Her breasts heaved up and down with each ragged breath.

He pressed one hand against her quivering stomach and kissed her neck as he bent her slightly over the dresser. "You're an amazing woman. Not only are you gorgeous, but you're smart and kind and as sweet as a cherry pie."

Her lips drew into a huge smile.

"Cherry pie was over the top, wasn't it?"

"Just a little." She gripped the dresser, arching her back and pressing firmly against him, making sure he buried himself deep inside her. She kept her gaze locked with his in the mirror. He nibbled on her ear while his fingers touched her intimately. Her eyelids grew heavy, and her toes curled. She shuddered.

His nostrils flared as he slammed inside her over and over again. It wasn't rough, but it wasn't gentle either. He groaned with each thrust. His face tightened, but he never stopped gazing into her eyes.

"Oh, my God," she managed as she convulsed against him. Her legs went weak, and she had to brace herself.

He grabbed her hips and squeezed tightly, pushing himself deep one last time. "Sage…beautiful Sage." He dotted her neck with tender kisses and smiled at her in the mirror.

At twenty-five, she hadn't expected to find a man that completely satisfied her physically, emotionally, and intellectually.

But everything she could want in a man came in the form of Porter Clayton.

Long moments ticked past as they stared at each other. His smile faded, and his face drained of color.

"What's the matter?" Fear gripped her throat and squeezed.

"Please tell me you're taking birth control pills."

"Every day except the last three because they are at home on my nightstand."

"Shit," he mumbled, taking a step back. "For as long

as I've been having sex, I've never once gone without a condom."

"Seriously? You've never had a relationship where she was the pill, and you didn't have to?"

"I wear one regardless, and for the record, I know I'm clean. Are you?" He dug in his drawer and pulled out a fresh pair of boxers and a t-shirt and handed them to her.

She took the clothes with a trembling hand. Quickly, she turned away and got dressed. Her mind filled with thoughts she didn't welcome, and her heart ached with a stabbing pain so sharp she wasn't sure she'd be able to fill her lungs. She didn't expect he'd want to have a relationship with her. That was ludicrous. He lived in Montana. In a trailer.

He didn't want a wife, much less a girlfriend.

And she didn't want to be...crap. She wanted it all.

But she'd never have it with him.

"Hey." He curled his fingers around her wrist and tugged her against his chest. "I didn't handle that very well."

"It's okay."

"No. It's not. You deserve better than me focusing on something I'm not concerned about. I know you're not the type of woman who sleeps around or would put someone else at risk. I am, however, utterly terrified that you could be pregnant and the fact that with you, I never want to wear a condom again. I had no idea how good that could be." He kissed her nose.

"You've turned my world upside down, and I'll never be the same."

She jumped when his phone rang. "Saved by the bell," she said, slipping from his embrace. "If we can get someone to stop by my place and get me some things, they can also bring my pills, and I can double up."

"But if you're pregnant, that could hurt the baby, right?"

"You do realize that your sperm probably hasn't made it to my egg, so there is no baby."

His dropped his gaze, and the right side of his mouth twitched. "I feel like I'm back in junior high school getting an erection during the sex education class."

# CHAPTER 8

CLAYTON STRETCHED out on the sofa and stared at the muted television while Sage finished up doing the dishes. Typically, he wouldn't want anyone in his kitchen, but since he cooked, she insisted, and hell, he couldn't say no to that woman if he tried.

The day had gone by quickly, which was good because it didn't give Clayton too much time to ponder Sage and whether or not he could have gotten her pregnant. He'd thought about having a vasectomy years ago, but since he'd always been so careful, why put himself through the torture.

In all his sexual years, he not once ever considered going without protection. He'd rather not have sex than take that risk, but he'd do it again with Sage. It wasn't just how his bare skin felt inside her, but what she did to his soul. She touched him in places he didn't know existed. He laughed. Kick told him that when he'd fallen in love, it happened so fast that even if he wanted to stop and run, he couldn't.

This wasn't love.

It couldn't be.

Heavy like? Sure.

Animal attraction? Absolutely.

Love? Good grief, he'd lost his mind.

The sound of an engine coming to a stop at the campsite across from his trailer caught his attention. He sat up and looked out the window. "My buddies are here."

"I hope they were able to get everything on my list."

Clayton laughed. "If they couldn't find it at Target, you ain't getting it."

She met him at the door and snapped the dishtowel at his leg.

He growled. "That hurt."

"Hurt so good."

She was going to be the death of him.

He gripped the handle. "Why don't you go into the bedroom. I'll bring everything back to you."

She lowered her chin and raised a brow. "Do you not want your friends—"

"Gawking at your sexy body? You're damn right I don't want that. Now scoot."

"Not on your life."

"Thank God they're both married," he mumbled as he pushed open the door. "Swede, Boomer, fancy meeting you here."

"I get a few days off to be with my family and what happens? You happen." Boomer slapped him on the shoulder as he breezed past him. "You must be Sage. It's a pleasure to meet you." He dropped a large Target bag on the floor and stretched out his hand. "I hope Mr. Dry-No-Personality is being a gentleman."

"Mr. Dry-No-Personality?" she asked, glancing between Clayton and Boomer.

"Clayton doesn't sweat under pressure, and he's the calmest man in combat I've ever served with," Swede said, holding out two smaller plastic bags. "I think we managed to get everything on your list."

"You two are lifesavers," she said.

"Hey, that's my job," Clayton teased with a wicked grin until Swede stared at him with a cocked head and a smirk. "Why don't you take all that stuff back to the bedroom."

"I hope the clothes fit and that you like them. My wife says I have shit taste," Swede said, making himself comfortable at the kitchen table.

"It's got to be better than wearing his clothes, which are ten sizes too big." She gathered up the bags and headed toward the bedroom. "I'll be out in a jiffy."

Clayton ducked his head into the fridge and pulled out three beers. "Let's take this outside."

"We brought marshmallows," Swede said with a little too much excitement.

"Tell me what you know." Once outside, Clayton went about making a small bonfire. As much as he wanted this over, he didn't want his time with Sage to end. Not yet, anyway.

"Trisha managed to get ahold of Stanley's phone records, and guess who has called him five times in the last two weeks."

"Maxwell." Clayton doused the wood with kerosene. He took the fire stick and set the logs ablaze. He stared at the yellow and orange flames inking toward the sky. "The man has been sentenced to life in prison without parole, and he's still fucking with my existence."

"It gets better," Swede said, taking a long draw from his beer. "Trisha also got into his email. It turns out Maxwell bankrolled a few deals for Stanley, forcing him to keep the businesses so Maxwell could launder his money."

"How long has that been going on?" Clayton sat on the log and fiddled with the condensation dripping down the side of his beer.

"About twenty years." Boomer took a small tablet out of his backpack. "Maxwell and Stanley went to high school together."

"No way." Clayton took the tablet in his hands and scrolled through the information.

"Their senior year a young woman was murdered by asphyxiation during a sex act," Boomer said. "It just happened to be Stanley's girlfriend at the time."

"Jesus," Clayton mumbled. While Sage had accepted her parents were a bit heartless, this might devastate her. "Why didn't that show up on a background check?"

"He was questioned and let go," Boomer said. "But he gave the cops a name." Boomer reached in front of Clayton and tapped the screen. "The cops arrested a man by the name of Jonathon Dixon who just happened to be Maxwell's stepfather."

"Maxwell's mother died in a car crash about the same time I left for the Navy. She wasn't married, and her name certainly wasn't Dixon." Clayton scratched the scruff on the side of his neck. "There was speculation that Maxwell had her killed, but I spoke to the lead on the case more than once, and he said Maxwell's hands were clean."

"Why would he have his own mother killed?" Swede asked.

"Same reason that he wants his son dead and will go to insane lengths to do it." Clayton chugged his beer. "He couldn't kill me at my mother's funeral, but his men tried. Anytime I set foot in Vegas, I'm looking over my shoulder waiting for someone like Nolan to show up and put a bullet in my back. I get the feeling that Maxwell is looking at killing two birds with one stone."

"So that brings us to something else Trisha uncovered," Swede said. "Maxwell sent images of Stanley having sex with Gina, the dead ex-girlfriend, and the time stamp is the night she died. The more Trisha dug, the more she believes Stanley killed his girlfriend, and Maxwell framed his stepfather for the deed."

"Alright, so Maxwell and Stanley are bound together in crime, but what does Sage have to do with all that?" There were too many unanswered questions, and every time they uncovered something, all it did was raise more questions. But it also showed Clayton the depths at which Stanley was hooked in tight with Maxwell, especially since their crimes seemed to go back to high school. Some bonds were nearly impossible to cut, something Clayton understood, but from a different angle. The deep connection he felt for his brothers both in and out of the military ran deep. He'd do anything for the men he'd served with, and he'd lay down his life for anyone in the Brotherhood Protectors. It was a code of honor that never needed to be spoken.

But now he found himself emotionally attached to Sage in ways he couldn't have imagined. It went beyond feeling protective, something he got paid to do. No. He cared for her in ways he didn't think he could.

And, if he were being honest, he wanted more. Hell, he wanted everything, and a huge part of him had been thrilled when his buddies didn't think it a good idea to go to her place.

That meant no birth control, and Clayton wasn't sure what to think about that.

He'd always believed he wasn't cut out to be a dad, but he wouldn't want to deny Sage the ability to have a family of her own. She might believe she didn't want that kind of traditional lifestyle, but Clayton saw the reality hidden in her soft sea-blue eyes. She had more love in her than he could have ever imagined. She was the kind of person he could only dream of being with.

"She's a means to get to you," Swede said. "Maxwell is using what he has over her parents to force their hand, and frankly, they only seem to think about themselves and making sure they come out smelling like roses. They don't care what happens to Sage."

"You're not telling me something, and I want to know what it is," Clayton said.

"Stanley contacted Glenn Nolan and gave him your location. The hit is scheduled to go down tonight," Boomer said. "Maxwell has been playing us all."

"It's time to turn the tables," Clayton said, setting his beer on the ground. "Let's put an end to this tonight."

"I'm glad you said that," Boomer said. "Trisha was able to track all of Stanley's calls today, and he spoke to Maxwell. He wants to kill Sage and make it look like you did it, and I will enjoy foiling that plan."

"I can't believe Maxwell would consider letting me live," Clayton said.

"Oh, he wants you to experience what prison life is like for a month or two before having someone kill you on the inside." Swede raised his beer. "Here's to putting Maxwell Busgy in his place."

"I'll drink to that," Clayton said. Now all he had to do was fill in the blanks with Sage and hope like hell she didn't freak out and change her mind because he was going to need her help to make sure her parents went to prison for their crimes.

"Are you okay?"

Sage tossed the tablet across the table. "What the fuck do you think?" She glared at Clayton. Coming to terms with her parents not loving her was one thing, but the fact they had no problem having her killed so her father wouldn't be called out as a murderer made her want to stick her head in the toilet.

"I wish it weren't true," Clayton said.

"You and me, both." She pulled out a chair and plopped her ass down. "If we manage to survive this plan, what will happen to my parents?"

"They will be arrested and most likely spend the rest of their lives in prison with my father."

"And if we fail?"

"You'll be dead, and I'll be visiting my father in prison so he can kill me himself."

"You know, I want to believe that my parents sent me off to boarding school to protect me from all this, but—"

"That might, in part, be true," Clayton said. He leaned against the kitchen sink, his weapon holstered on his belt.

"My foundation is tainted now." Every penny her father had loaned her was blood money, and that just made her sick to her stomach. At this point, she'd rather be living on the streets than taking a single dime from her father.

"No. It's not. And don't you dare ever stop going the extra mile. The world needs people like you."

"Right. Because asking my criminal father to bankroll a charity is such a noble thing."

"Hey, my mom stole from Maxwell to start the Alley Home, and I'd do the same thing. Hell, if I could find a way for you to have all your parents' money and use it for something good, then all this would be well worth it."

"All I've ever wanted was for them to be proud of me. To love and support me." She lifted a wine glass to her lips and took a big gulp.

"I love and support you."

The glass slipped from her fingers, shattering on the floor. "What did you just say?"

"I think what you are doing is amazing. You've helped more people in your fundraising endeavors than any other not-for-profit. That's something to be proud of." Clayton snagged the broom and dustpan and went about cleaning up the broken pieces of glass around her feet.

"And I am, but it's the front part of your original statement that has my pulse raging to dangerous levels." Love? Did he feel something akin to love? Granted, he didn't say he loved her, but he did use the damn stupid word.

After tossing the glass into the trash, he glanced to the ceiling as if he searched for an answer he didn't already have.

"Let me help you," she said, taking in a deep breath for support. "You used the word love, and while I have your attention, why was there a pregnancy test in the bag of crap your buddies brought me?"

He stood and inched his way into her personal space. She should run, and run fast, but instead, she caved to her need to be touched.

Caressed.

Cared for.

Fuck. She wanted desperately to have him love her for real.

"They say you can find out if you're pregnant long before you've missed a period, and I think it's important for us to know."

"Why?" She raised her palms. "So we can make the same mistakes our parents did?"

"You aren't anything like your mom and dad, and you've helped me see how it doesn't matter who my birth father was. I'm a decent person who, in the end, does the right thing."

She tossed her head back and laughed. "Of course, you're a decent man, but that has nothing to do with the fact neither one of us are prepared to take care of a little human, much less want to." Only, if she were carrying his child, she'd want to keep it. She'd want to raise it and love it like it was the most extraordinary thing that ever happened.

As children should be seen in the eyes of their parents.

"I don't see what's so funny," he said.

"The likelihood I'm pregnant is slim to none, but that's not even half of what I'm laughing at." She cleared her throat. He deserved for her to act like the grown-up she was, even if everything felt utterly absurd. "I'm sorry, this isn't anything to laugh at, but seriously, I'm completely turning on my parents. They might not have honestly loved me, but they did provide for me, and this feels icky."

"Icky is one way to put it, but remember they have no problem having you murdered to save their own collective assess." He shoved a tablet in front of her. "These emails don't lie."

She tapped the screen and scanned the documents that proved without a doubt that her father was indeed in bed with organized crime. Her mother was more than a corporate lawyer; she helped get many of their associates off, and she had done her best to hide criminal activity.

But there was no denying that Maxwell ordered a hit on her and wanted to make it look like Clayton had done it. If they didn't do their part, then Maxwell would toss them under the bus. Her parents would end up bankrupt and facing criminal charges.

Clayton's cell rang, cutting through the thick tension.

"Hey, Dustin, you're on speaker with Sage."

"I've got good news and bad news. What do you want first?" Dustin asked.

"God, I hate that question," Sage mumbled.

Clayton paced in front of the table with his hands on his hips. His feet rattled the floorboards. The sound of his buddies sitting outside by the campfire tickled her ears. She was in good hands, and they had a plan to not only protect her but to bring down her parents. Unfortunately, she'd overheard Clayton telling Boomer and Swede that they needed more time to gather enough evidence to prove her parents' role in all this and more.

Otherwise, she still might end up dumped in the desert, only to end up like a crisp piece of chicken.

"Always the good news first," Clayton said.

"Nolan is on his way toward the campground. Estimated time of arrival is in twenty-eight minutes."

She didn't know why that was good news, but it made Clayton smile like a little boy.

"Let the party begin," Clayton said. "Now, bring on the bad."

"I'm not sure you want to do this on speaker—"

"She has the right to know, especially since we're putting her in danger." Clayton stopped pacing for a second.

Usually, she hated people speaking for her, but in

this instance, she was perfectly fine with it. She nodded.

"All right," Dustin said. "Stanley and Lorna are about to make a press statement."

"About what?" Clayton practically jumped over the coffee table. He managed to find the remote and pointed it at the television.

"They officially fired us, so everything we're getting is through illegal means, but they are going to announce that their daughter is being held for ransom by you."

"That's an interesting twist, but the Brotherhood will back me, so kind of a stupid plan."

"Not really," Dustin said. "They have footage of you ramming into the Lyft driver, and then you shooting Weslynn and—"

"That's impossible," Sage said.

"It's pretty easy to forge a fake video, which will eventually be found out, but you know how things go viral," Clayton said as if he had nothing to worry about.

Tears stung her eyes. She folded her arms over her chest.

Clayton kneeled in front of her, taking her hands into his strong ones. "It's going to be okay. I won't let anything happen to you."

"If you don't manage to take down my parents, I'm ruined. You take them down. I'm ruined. Everything I've worked for will be gone in a snap of a finger. The money for my foundation will be called—"

"Sage. I told you I'd be by your side every step of the way. I will keep you alive and make sure you can still do all the wonderful work your charity has been doing for the last few years. I promise."

She cupped his face. No man she'd ever met had the kind of honor that Clayton had. He was the real deal. He was everything she could ever want in a man.

He pressed his lips against hers for a brief kiss. It was soft and tender.

Loving.

"If this goes bad I want to say thank —"

"It's not going to go bad, so save any thoughts you have for when all this is done, and I have the chance to take you on a proper date."

"If things go well, there will be nothing proper about it."

# CHAPTER 9

"I CAN'T BELIEVE I agreed to this." Clayton sat on the log in front of the firepit with his weapon in his lap. A nearly full moon glowed brightly in the star-dotted sky. Every op came with risks, but there was nothing worse than using a civilian as bait.

"Can't say I'm thrilled either." Sage sat on the ground between his legs. She tucked her knees to her chest. "I don't see we have any other choice."

"There are other options, but they aren't any better." He ran his fingers through her soft hair, careful not to tug too hard. Being with her was the most natural thing in the world. He liked the idea of taking her inside and snuggling up against her back while they lay in bed watching a movie. Sitting with a woman for hours, doing nothing but being with each other hadn't been something Clayton had any desire to do.

But with Sage, everything was different.

"I feel like I have a red dot on the center of my chest." Sage dropped her head back and hugged his thigh. She glanced up at him with sadness, stuck in her sweet eyes. "And what my father said about you during the press conference…I'm so sorry."

Clayton shrugged. "I've been called a bastard my entire life."

"He spewed lies about you and the kind of man you are."

"Not all of them are lies."

"You're aren't holding me against my will, and that is so not the point," she said. "People will believe them, especially since my father told the world that Maxwell is your biological dad."

"I don't care what anyone thinks of me." How he wished that statement were true. It was one thing to accept Maxwell had fathered him, but it was another thing to admit how that fact made Clayton feel about himself.

A whore for a mother.

A gangster for a father.

The former he wasn't ashamed of, the latter made him sick to his stomach. His mother never intentionally hurt anyone. She did what she had to in order to survive. Only she continued to work as an escort even when she didn't have to.

It took Clayton a long time to accept his mother couldn't or wouldn't give up a half a dozen of her regular clients. These men were kind to his mother and lavished her in gifts and money, much like Maxwell had, only they didn't force his mother to give it all back or beat her into submission.

But still, his mother never stopped selling her body, and he had to admit, if only to himself, that fact bothered him, but only because Clayton knew in the depths of his soul what he was capable of doing.

And that wasn't any better than his gangster father.

Clayton's genetics were not something that should be passed on to another generation.

"You're lying," Sage said with an authoritative and all-knowing tone. "You care very deeply what others think of you, or you wouldn't be so aloof and live in a trailer that can be attached or detached from your truck at any minute. You choose not to get close to people because you're afraid they might find out that you believe you are no better than your father. Maybe in some ways, your mother as well."

He waggled his finger. "I loved my mom."

"I'm not saying you don't. I loved…love my parents." She swiped her finger under her eye. "When it comes out what my parents have done, the world will look at me differently."

He cupped her cheeks and held her gaze. "No. You're innocent in all this, and everyone will see that."

"You're innocent as well—"

"I've done some bad things in my day."

"Like what?" she asked.

"I've had to take human life."

"Had to? During combat? To save yourself and others? That doesn't make you a bad person," she said with fire in her throaty voice.

"You don't know the half of it. And if you did, you would think very differently of me." He wanted to push from her sweet touch and tender gaze. It had been twenty-five years since he'd uttered a single word about what could have destroyed his life. Hell, he barely allowed himself to think about it. Had Frost not stood in Clayton's corner all those years ago, Clayton could have easily been sharing a cell with his father.

"While we're waiting to be attacked, why don't you tell me," she said.

Being honest with her might make it easier for both of them to say goodbye because she wouldn't be able to look at him once she knew the truth. "It's an ugly story."

"What is it you think you've done that is so bad?"

"I killed someone." He pressed his fingers over her lips. "It wasn't in combat. I was fifteen years old."

Her eyes widened, and her jaw slacked open.

His heart beat so fast that he had trouble filling his lungs. A wave of nausea gripped his stomach. He hadn't let his mind go back and pull up the images from that day since his mother's funeral. He'd filed them in a back corner of his brain and did his best to forget.

She cleared her throat. "Are you going to leave me hanging?"

"Do you really want to know?"

She nodded.

He shifted his gaze to the fire, flickering toward the sky. The yellow, orange, and red flames swirled and merged, snapping his memory into focus. Clutching his chest, he heaved in a deep breath. Telling her would give her the freedom to walk away from him and never look back. It would be hard, considering what was about to happen to her parents, but he couldn't bear the thought of keeping her down, and that would be exactly what he'd do if he even attempted to have something with her when all was said and done.

"There was this girl I was dating when I was in high school. Her name was Bella, and she was the prettiest girl I'd ever seen at that time." Clayton slid from the log to the ground, sitting next to her, but keeping a safe distance. He needed to remain detached from it all, or he might fall apart, and he couldn't afford to do that. "She grew up much like I had, but her mom had married some rich dude and took them from the streets. He didn't like me. Didn't think I was good enough for Bella, so he forbid her to see me."

"You said you killed someone. Can we get to that part of the story, please?"

Her words stung his heart, but it was the way she looked at him with a dash of understanding behind her shocked-filled eyes that terrified him.

"She came to school one day with a black eye. She told me she walked into a door, but I knew better.

When I pressed her, I found she had bruises in other places, and she told me her stepfather had raped her."

Sage gasped, covering her mouth. "What did you do?"

"I went to her house and confronted him." Clayton ripped open his shirt, pulling it down over his shoulder. "If you look carefully, you'll see a scar from a bullet here." He tapped his tattoo and then turned his back. "And another one on the Eagle's head."

Her fingers burned his skin as she traced the scar. "He shot you, and you killed him in self-defense."

"Unfortunately, he wasn't the only one who died that day."

"Bella?"

"When she told me at school, I just took off with rage in my heart. I wanted him to die, and I wanted to be the man to kill him."

"You wanted him to pay, but you didn't want him dead."

"Oh, yes, I did. To me, he represented every man who hit a woman, or a prostitute, or anyone for that matter. He represented all the bad things that created my world, and I wanted it to end. I wanted more for Bella. And for myself. But Bella followed me, and the bullet that hit my back had gone right through her body before nailing me. She died in my arms."

"You didn't kill her."

"I might not have pulled the trigger, but she's dead

143

because I acted out of emotion, something I won't ever do again."

"You're kidding, right? Because he would have killed her, anyway."

"Nope. Because I killed him too." Clayton had heard this argument a million times, including from all the first responders that had shown up that day. Not to mention, Clayton had never been charged for a single crime, even though he thought he should have been. He'd already suspected Maxwell was his father, so Bella's death just gave him the proof that the apple didn't fall far from the tree.

He should have been arrested because he showed no mercy.

He hated putting Sage through this, but if he didn't, he feared he'd want to find a way to keep her in his life, and that wouldn't be good.

"You're not giving me all the facts," Sage said. Tears rolled down her cheeks. "And he raped a young girl, he—"

"He deserved a fair trial, but he didn't get that because after he shot Bella and me, I managed to stab him twice. The second time I hit a main artery, and he bled out before help got there."

"That's self-defense," she said.

"I went after him. I threw the first punch. He was the one defending himself."

"Do you feel guilty?" she asked.

That wasn't a question anyone had ever asked him

before. As a matter of fact, everyone told him not to feel bad. But no one asked him how he felt about it.

"I feel guilty human life was lost."

"Do you feel guilty for defending your friend?"

"No," he admitted. "But my actions directly caused her death."

"Well, if anyone raped and beat me, I hope I have someone like you on my side. And for the record, that doesn't make you like your father. If anything, it makes you the exact opposite."

The microphone in his ear crackled.

"We've got Nolan, only it's not Nolan," Boomer said. "We'll be there in five."

He tapped his ear. "Who is it, then?" Clayton's lungs deflated. They were playing a risky game, but it was the only way to bring Stanley down without having to spend months, maybe even years, gathering information, only to have him get off on a technicality. If they could pin him on conspiracy to commit murder, they suspected shortly after, the DA would be able to dig deeper and put Stanley behind bars for life.

But where did that leave Sage? She might be strong, smart, and perfectly capable of taking care of herself, but this would forever change her life, and he was partially to blame.

"It's an interesting story and one best told in person. However, the plan is still the same, so it's time to have Sage take cover."

"Ten-four," he said, turning his attention back to Sage. "I want you to go in the trailer, okay?"

"Why? What's going on?"

"Just do it and lock the door," he said behind a tight jaw. None of this was her fault, and since he believed that, he had to believe it wasn't his fault either.

Caring about someone put a damper on his ability to be dishonest with himself.

"You're scaring me," she said.

He jumped to his feet, pulling her with him. "This should all be over in the next half hour, so just go inside and try to relax."

"Easy for you to say."

He held her hands, rubbing his thumbs over her skin. "Do you trust me?"

She nodded.

"Good." He kissed her gently, lovingly. He kissed her as if she were the air that he breathed. "We're going to be okay."

He watched her step into his trailer. She glanced over her shoulder. Tears shimmered across her cheeks.

"Wait for my signal," he said.

"Be safe." She blew him a kiss.

"Always." After the door closed, he tossed a few more logs on the fire and poked at them. The next few minutes ticked by slowly as he waited for Boomer.

In the distance, he could see Boomer walking up the road, his rifle slung over his shoulder as another man stepped out in front of him, his arms swinging freely.

That gave Clayton pause.

"What's going on?" he asked.

"Clayton, meet very special agent Benny Young," Boomer said. "They picked up Nolan a couple of hours ago. It looks like your girl's friend hacked his arm so good that he had to seek medical attention. He went to a vet who called the Feds, so he's been in custody for the last twenty-four hours."

"That pretty much fucks up our plan." Clayton shook Benny's hand. "Why'd you have Sage take cover if Nolan isn't here?"

"Because her father thinks I'm Nolan," Benny said. "And we didn't think she needed to hear everything I had to say before we move forward."

If this were any other job, he'd agree and go alone, but this wasn't just any case, and Sage was his charge. "No. If you have something to say about her father, she has the right to know."

"He's taken a hit out on his own kid. That's way too much—"

"She knows that already." Clayton made his way to the trailer and pounded on the door. "Sage. Come on out."

"It's more than that," Benny said. "It's too dangerous for her to know."

"I agree." Boomer held up his hand. "But if she were my girl, I'd want her to hear the truth before it comes out in a media shitstorm she might not recover from."

"Have it your way," Benny said.

A couple of seconds later, Sage stuck her head out. "What's going on?"

Clayton took her by the hand and led her back to the firepit. "I'm not exactly sure, but this is Benny. He's a federal agent."

"Now I'm totally wigged out," Sage said.

"Sorry to meet you under these circumstances," Benny said as he leaned against Clayton's truck.

"So, can we cut to the chase?" Clayton asked, keeping his arm looped around Sage's waist, holding her steady.

"In a nutshell, the man hired to kidnap Sage has been taken into custody, and we cut a deal with him—"

"Of course you did." Clayton cut Benny off. "I'm well aware of how Nolan operates; now, can we get to the problem at hand?" Clayton didn't like it when someone else called the shots on his operation, but he knew his hands were tied, and his job was to protect Sage, and he'd do whatever it took to make sure she walked away without even a scratch on her head.

"Stanley has no idea what Nolan looks like," Benny said.

"Are you sure about that?" Clayton knew better than anyone that Nolan kept a low profile, not wanting most people to know what he looked like. It had been joked that Nolan was a master of disguise, and Clayton didn't doubt that, but people did know who he looked like.

And Clayton was one of those people.

"We're sure." Benny took one of the chairs and made himself comfortable in front of the fire. "Funny thing is, we've had our eye on Stanley, his company, and his wife's firm now for a while, but it wasn't until after we picked up Nolan that we found out Stanley wanted to hire him for a second job."

"To kill me." Sage shivered.

Clayton pulled her close and pressed his lips against her temple. "No one is going to kill you on my watch."

"Or mine," Benny said.

"Me three," Boomer chimed in with a grin.

"Anyway, we'd like to alter the plan," Benny said.

"Alter, how?" Clayton never liked last-minute adjustments. "Why can't we stage her death, making me look as though I did it to force Stanley to confess."

"That won't give us enough to shut him and his wife down," Benny said.

"What did my parents do, exactly?" Sage stiffened her spine and stood taller.

"A plethora of things between embezzling money, laundering money, fraud, to name a few. The bigger crime we want them on is human trafficking."

"Excuse me?" Sage's voice cracked.

"I'm sure you've seen the news lately about missing prostitutes?"

"Fuck," Clayton muttered. "How are they involved in that?" He'd seen all the news reports on the missing girls, half were thought to be runaway teens, the other half most figured they moved on, but hookers didn't just move on. Life on the streets didn't work that way. They needed help to get out of that way of life, and as his mother knew all too well, it was almost impossible to stay away. Of course, his mother said she did so to ensure she helped as many women and their kids as she could, even if that meant keeping a foothold in that way of life.

Sage shook her head. "No. No. No way. My parents might be a lot of things, but trafficking young girls? I don't believe it."

"I wish I could tell you it wasn't true, but one of the many business holdings your parents own is a talent agency, but it's also a cover for getting young girls and boys out of the country and sold into slavery."

"Are you talking about the Holland Agency?" Clayton asked.

Benny nodded.

"Fuck. Right before my mother died, she told me about her concerns over missing hookers and their connection to the Holland Agency. Nothing ever came of it, and I let it go."

"My parents wouldn't…wouldn't…" Sage's voice trailed off. She glanced up at him. "That's not your fault."

Leave it to her to switch her focus to him and not the pain her own parents caused her. Clayton squeezed her hip. Her entire world had been turned upside down all because she wanted her father to be proud of her accomplishments; only her father turned out to be unworthy of Sage's loyalty.

"Are you positive about what my parents have been doing?" Sage's voice turned hard and cold.

There was nothing Clayton could do to stop the change happening in Sage's mental state. He might not have been exactly where she stood, but he understood betrayal in more ways than one.

"We've been trying to nail your father ever since he took over for Maxwell."

Clayton groaned. He should have known Maxwell had a hand in all this. "And what does Maxwell say about Stanley and this operation."

"He's the one who gave us all the information."

"That sounds like a setup to me," Boomer said as he poked at one of the logs with a long stick. "What does he get out of it?"

"Payback," Benny said. "Stanley and Lorna made the mistake of thinking that just because Maxwell was in prison, that meant they could run the operations any way they wanted."

"So, he's yanking their chain to get rid of me and destroy them in the process," Clayton said."

"You've got that one right," Benny said. "Maxwell doesn't care how any of this goes down as long as the Adams' pay for stealing and Clayton either ends up dead or blamed for a murder."

Clayton wondered if he'd ever be out from under Maxwell's curse. He thought by denying the man was his father, he'd be free of his grasp, especially since Maxwell had told him to his face that Clayton wasn't good enough to be his kin.

That was fine by Clayton.

But the reality was that Maxwell's blood raced through Clayton's veins, and as long as Clayton continued to give the man space in his brain, Maxwell would always be a part of his life, and that was something he could no longer accept. If he was going to have any chance at the kind of life he realized he wanted, it was time to stop giving Maxwell space inside his brain.

"How can we help make sure my parents go to jail?" Sage asked.

"Instead of faking your death, we want you to wear a wire and get them talking," Benny said.

"Over my dead body," Clayton interjected.

"That can be arranged because we think they are more apt to talk if they think you're dead. Maxwell has all but said he doesn't care who dies, as long as you get blamed for it," Benny said. "So, you die, and we put a wire on her, and she gets her parents to tell us all about where they are hiding the missing young men and women and when the next sale is and to whom."

"No way. I won't allow it," Clayton said. "It's too dangerous."

Sage poked his arm. "I'm doing it."

"Babe, it's—"

"Time to get my hands dirty," Sage with a tinge of pride.

"That's not what I meant when I said that." Clayton closed the gap, ignoring the two men right behind him. He took her chin between his thumb and forefinger, tilting her head. Her soft blue eyes caught the glow of the moon, making his knees go weak.

"My parents are bad people, and I couldn't live with myself if I just sat back and did nothing. That young woman who thought being the person in the middle of check writers and those in need no longer exists. The woman you see standing in front of you right now takes action to help people, and right now, I can do something to stop one more girl from becoming another statistic."

The corners of his mouth tipped upward. His heart swelled with pride. "We do this only if I get to listen and be armed and ready to go in and take those pieces of shit down."

"I can live with that," Benny said.

"Good," Clayton said, leaning closer to Sage's ear. "Love and support. That's what you get from me from now on."

# CHAPTER 10

SAGE RACED THROUGH THE TRAILER, slamming into the bathroom door. She wiggled the handle, praying it opened before she made a complete fool of herself.

Gagging and coughing, she dropped to her knees in front of the toilet and hurled. Her stomach twisted and gurgled, and her mind couldn't erase the image of Clayton lying on the floor, eyes glazed over, with fake blood pooling all around his limp body. It didn't matter that none of it was real; it was still burned permanently in her mind.

She rested her forehead on her arm and tried to breathe slowly and methodically.

"Hey, you," Clayton's calm voice eased the ache in her heart.

"Are you still covered in blood?" The worst part had been watching a streak of fake blood dribble out of Clayton's mouth while they continued to stage his murder. Flashes of light had filled the tiny trailer while Boomer and Swede documented the crime with their phone.

"A little." He slid down to the floor and rested his hand on her back, massaging gently. "Are you sure you want to go through with this?"

With as much dignity as she could muster, she lifted her head and brushed her hair from her face. "I need to do it. Besides, having a bit of a weak stomach might help with my performance."

"I'm sorry about your parents."

"Me too." She pushed from the toilet. Her hands shook violently. She pumped her fingers in and out, creating fists each time.

Clayton helped her to a standing position, holding her firmly at the shoulders. He stared into her eyes, taking her breath away.

She tried to swallow, but her throat wouldn't work correctly.

"I'm going be less than a mile away, and if you need me to come crashing in, you know the code words."

She nodded. "Your full name, Porter Clayton."

He let out a slight chuckle. "No one calls me that, and it sounds so weird."

"Porter's a nice name."

"It was the last name of the doctor who delivered me. My mom thought if I was going to be burdened with a first name for a last name, I might as well have a last name for a first name."

"That's a mouth full," she said with a slight smile. "And I don't think I could call you Porter now if I tried."

"Good, because I've been Clayton since I could talk." He leaned in and kissed her plump lips. "I find myself caring about you more than anyone else I've ever known," he whispered against her ear.

Closing her eyes, she rested her head against his shoulder. "My entire existence has changed in a blink of an eye. After today, I probably don't even have a home, since my parents own it, or should I say, one of their illegal holdings—"

"You can stay with me for as long as you need. Love and support, remember?"

"What does that even mean?" She jerked her head back and blinked away the cobwebs that had taken up residence in her mind. "I get you're here for me for as long as I'm paying...shit, I don't know if I'll even have a dime after this. I mean, all my money came from my parents, including my foundation."

"Stop talking," Clayton said.

She snapped her lips closed and glared.

"I don't work for you."

"When my father—"

He hushed her with a quick swirl of his tongue in her mouth. If the kiss hadn't knocked her socks off, she would have protested.

"I'm not your hired bodyguard. I won't take a dime from you or anyone else to protect you."

"I'm not sure your boss will agree with that."

Clayton smiled. "We took the initial down payment from your dad. That's all he needs. Besides, I'm still technically on vacation for another week."

"And this is what you want to do with your spare time?"

"If it means I get more time with you, then yes."

"You're a confusing man, and you still haven't answered my original question."

"Love and support means exactly what it sounds like. I'm here for you, no matter what. I won't leave your side, and I'm hoping that you want to explore whatever is going on with us by taking a little road trip with me when this is all said and done."

"Are you joking? You want me to ride off into the sunset in your camper after I put my parents in jail?" The moment the words left her mouth, she realized that was exactly what she wanted.

Needed.

He cocked his head but said nothing as if he knew what she was thinking.

And that scared her more than anything.

"We don't have to go anywhere. I'll do whatever you need."

"Why do you have to be so sweet. It was easier when I thought you were an aloof cowboy who probably had a liking for prostitutes."

"Well, I do have a liking for them; I just don't fancy them."

She poked him in the chest. "You are so not funny, and that so won't get you laid either."

"I'm just glad I'm in the running for the latter." He kissed her nose. "And for the record, I'll do whatever it takes to make sure your charity foundation doesn't take too big of a hit. If it does, then I have some money hidden away you can use."

"I can't take your money."

"Of course you can. Besides, my mother took it from Maxwell, and no, I don't think it's tainted at all, especially if it's backing a good cause, and you, my lovely lady, are the only person I want to put my time, energy, and money behind."

"Love and support," she said softly.

"Exactly," he said.

"Okay, you two," Boomer called. "We need to get this party started."

"Let's get this over with," Sage said.

THE TAPE STICKING to Sage's chest itched her skin, making her want to crawl right out of it. A bead of sweat dotted her forehead. They had gone over the plan a dozen times since Benny sent her parents the text message along with images that things hadn't gone quite as planned and that their daughter had been the one to kill Clayton.

She slammed on the brakes as she pulled into her

parents' driveway, stopping just short of the big cast-iron gate. Leaning out the window, she hit the pin code on the keypad. The gate rattled, sliding open. The large tree branches swayed in the gentle breeze. The leaves danced over the stars and the moon.

Staring at her childhood home, she realized she needed a map to find her way around. This wasn't her home. It had never been, and it never will be. She wondered if her parents still kept a room for her, though she doubted it since her parents hadn't let her stay the night since her junior year in high school. She'd always thought that strange, but never thought it would be because of criminal activity. No, she just thought she was unlovable.

*Love and support.*

Clayton's words bounced around her brain like a rubber ball, pinging here, landing there, hitting her over and over again that she'd been looking for love and support in all the wrong places, only she never expected it to happen with him.

Not in a million years.

She eased closer to the enormous house. Only a few outside lights were shining in the night. One of the four-car garage doors was open, and a silhouette stood in the entrance.

She took in a deep breath and let it out slowly. If this worked, her parents would go away for a long time.

If it failed, she could be dead, or worse, on the run from a bunch of mobsters.

Her father stepped into the light and waved her forward. Her heart hammered in her chest. She glanced down at her shaking hands, which were covered in blood. All she had to do was get her parents to believe she killed Clayton to save her parents from going to prison.

That was probably the easy part.

The hard part would be getting her parents to tell her where the missing boys and girls were as well as confessing more of their crimes.

"You've put me in a tough situation." Her father yanked opened the driver's door. "What the hell were you thinking?"

She took in a deep breath and stepped from the vehicle. "It's not like I meant to do it. But what's done is done, and I need to know if you're going to help me."

"Get in the house." He slammed the car door. "Is that blood?"

"That sometimes happens when you kill someone." She stepped into the kitchen where her mother sat at the island with a bottle of whiskey by her side.

"This isn't how this was supposed to go down," her mother said.

"And exactly what were you expecting to happen?" Sage asked.

Her mother's icy glare sent a cold ripple across Sage's skin. She'd always been slightly terrified of the woman, but looking at her now, Sage wanted to vomit. Her mother had never loved her, and she never would.

"We're just glad you're okay."

"Right," her mother said with a sarcastic laugh. "So, the bastard's dead, huh?" Her mother raised her glass to the air. The ice clinked, and the brown liquid sloshed up the sides. Her mother had always had an abrasive personality. Some might describe her as cold, and Sage wouldn't disagree. Sage couldn't remember a time when her mother had been warm and fuzzy. Hugs and kisses weren't part of their family traditions. Actually, they had not a single tradition. In all Sage's twenty-five years on this planet, she probably spent only a handful of holidays with her family. During those visits, the media were invited, or there was some major event her parents had to attend, which meant so did Sage, but only for a photo op and once that obligation was met, Sage was sent packing.

"You saw the pictures." Sage made a beeline for the sink. She glanced at her trembling hands, and a vision of Clayton lying on the ground filled her mind. She kept telling herself it wasn't real, but the blood looked and felt real. She flipped on the faucet and let the warm water race over her hands. Red tacky liquid filled the basin.

"I can't believe you, of all people, killed that vile creature." Her mother continued to sip her whiskey.

"It was either him or me." Sage snagged the bottle of booze and brought it to her lips. She took a big gulp, shocked that the burning didn't make her gag or choke. "Tell me, Dad, what do you know about Glenn Nolan?" Usually, small talk was about all she and her parents could handle, but today, she needed to get right down to business.

She coughed on her last gulp of whiskey.

Her father cleared his throat. "I hired him to get you and Weslynn out of harm's way when I got that threatening note from Rotork."

"Daddy, stop lying to me. We both know that Rotork had nothing to do with it, and Nolan was there to kidnap and murder me."

"How dare you accuse your father of such things," her mother said.

"I'm accusing both of you," Sage said under her breath. "I know you hired Nolan to get me out of the way so you could set Clayton up for a plethora of crimes. But that plan has gone to shit, and now Clayton is dead, and I have blood on my hands." She flicked her wrists a few times before grabbing a towel. She held the terrycloth in her hands, staring at the image of a pineapple. "I killed a man, so please, tell me why."

"There is nothing to tell," her mother said. "And that is for your own good. Had you just stayed in France, in the condo your father bought you, none of this would have happened."

"Seriously, Mom? That's what you believe? That man I just killed has video of Dad murdering a young woman years ago. He had proof that the two of you kidnap and sell young girls and boys to the highest bidder. And he had proof of the business dealings you both have with Maxwell Busgy, who is in prison right now. So, please, I'm begging, tell me what we're dealing with, so I can help make sure we don't go down for any of it."

"We?" Her mother tossed her head back and laughed. "There is no we. Your father and I did nothing wrong."

"Like hell, you haven't. I'm not blind, and for the past three years, I've been watching, and I can tell you, so have the Feds."

Her mother's laugh was cut short. "Is that what the piece of shit, Clayton, told you? That man is the son of a whore."

"That whore used to sleep with Dad." Sage gagged on the words, but not because she was disgusted by Clayton's mother. Far from it. She still didn't agree with her actions, but it was her father that was the real criminal in this scenario.

Her mother slammed her glass on the island. An ice cube flipped out onto the counter. "What else did that bastard tell you? Did he tell you that woman was black-mailing your father so he'd continue to give her money?"

"Dad was only paying for services rendered, right, Dad?" Sage had been told to be prepared for lies upon lies. That she should expect redirection and deflections, but that she should, no matter what, try to stick with the script.

Fuck that.

She knew it wouldn't work.

"I told you that fucking whore would be your downfall," her mother said. "Her pussy must have had superpowers because she had a dozen powerful men dropping at her feet."

Sage shivered.

"Shut up, Lorna. She's been dead for ten years. She has no pull over me anymore. But Maxwell is still yanking our chains. He's the person we need to deal with."

"He's only half the problem, and it's the Feds you should be worried about. If you want my help—"

"Help? Child, you're the one that needs our help. There's a dead man in a trailer at a campsite, and it can be proven that you were there with him. Hell, you drove here in a dead Clayton's vehicle," her mother said. "Even if you can convince someone it was in self-defense, you still ended a man's life. Your father and I had nothing to do with that."

"There are two men dead in the trailer." Sage needed to move things along. She wasn't sure she could continue with this charade much longer.

"You killed someone else?" her mother asked with a humorous kick to her words. "I don't believe it."

"I didn't kill him. Clayton did. It turns out he was a hitman there to kill me. Actually, he's the same man who tried to kidnap me. Any idea who might have hired a contract killer on me?"

"Maxwell," both her parents stated at the same time.

"Now, why would a man I don't know want me dead?" Sage asked.

"He's doing whatever he can to destroy us, as well as his own son. Maxwell cares only about himself," her father said.

"That might be true." Sage knew Maxwell had a hand in the insanity of her current situation, but it was her parents who had hired Nolan, and it was her parents who were currently trafficking young girls and boys. It was her parents who needed to go down, and that's who she'd focus on. "But you should know that the Brotherhood Protector group has a shit-ton of information about the next load to be sold off, so we have to move the merchandise, or all three of us will end up in prison and most likely facing the death penalty."

"Jesus Christ." Her mother poured another hefty glass of whiskey.

"What exactly did Clayton tell you?" her father asked.

"His boss had a meeting with a federal agent who was given information about *our* human trafficking operation by Maxwell."

"What the hell are you talking about?" her mother asked. "That is just an ugly lie."

"Mom, we have to act fast, or nothing any of us say

or do will keep us from going to prison. I don't think you want that."

"Fuck," her mother muttered.

"I was able to get Clayton to give up some information before I killed him. He said that Maxwell gave the authorities the location for the next pickup, as well as a list of current buyers and that the Feds are days from closing in. That was yesterday." Sage took another good hit of the whiskey. It burned her stomach but warmed her brain. "If you want to keep your business going, I suggest we move the merchandise now. Once the cops find Clayton's body, we need to have made sure that any information he gave the Feds doesn't pan out and have a good reason for why I was here with you since early this morning, and not with him."

"Since when did you become so assertive," her mother said, stepping from behind the counter. In her right hand, she held a small handgun.

Sage swallowed.

Hard.

"You've always been such a little people pleaser, needing everyone's approval. What changed?" her father asked. "And you haven't once mentioned how you plan on making sure you don't go away for murder, why is that?"

"Clayton and Nolan got into a gunfight; they killed each other."

"That's not going to fly," her father said, not denying

ROUGH EDGE

anything. "I came out on national television and said that Clayton all but kidnapped my kid."

"I didn't see that," Sage lied, surprised that her father went there as quickly as he did. Clayton had been so sure of how her father would focus on that, but Sage wasn't so sure.

She'd been wrong.

About a lot of things.

"We can use that to our advantage," her mother said, still holding the weapon between her fingers. "Call Ron at the warehouse. Have him send someone over to the trailer and make sure what Sage says is all true."

"I sent you pictures. Do you need to see them again?" Sage asked.

"No." Her mother held the gun in the air, pointing at Sage's shoulder.

She shifted to the right.

And so did her mother.

Fuck.

"Where are you keeping the young prostitutes you kidnapped?" Sage pursed her lips and stared directly into her mother's cold eyes.

Her mother stepped into Sage's personal space and pressed the nozzle of the weapon against Sage's temple.

"Lorna, what the hell are you doing?" Sage's father asked.

"Tell me something, daughter dearest, do you think we're that stupid?" her mother asked.

"No. I think you're that crazy." Sage did her best to

remain calm. Growing up, she barely knew her mother, but she had it in her head that her mom was kind and loving, just busy, and into her career.

Ha.

Talk about delusional.

"The Feds are onto you, and unless you move the merchandise now, you'll be arrested by the end of the day tomorrow." In all her years, she'd never once spoken back to her parents, much less allowed her natural sarcasm to shine through.

Sage no longer cared about her parents or what they thought. "Are you housing the young men and women in the warehouse? Or somewhere else?"

"Why would we tell you that?" Her mother held her gaze, the gun still way too close for comfort.

"Lorna put the gun down. She's on our side," her father said.

"You've always had a soft spot for her, but I told you she would never have what it takes to be part of our organization, and I've waited too long for Maxwell to go down to screw it up now." Her mother waved the handgun in the air. "Since the man we hired to kill you fucked up, I'm going to have to do what I should have done the day I found out I was pregnant with you."

"Lorna," her father said with a stiff upper lip. "Shut the fuck up, and let's think this through."

"I'm trying to help," Sage said. Her confidence faltered. "Clayton checks in with his team every morning, first thing. When they don't hear from him, they will come running. I can only assume that the Feds—"

"Don't assume, child." Her mother poked her in the chest with the gun.

The metal from the microphone dug into her skin. She winced.

"You little bitch." Her mother rammed her hand between Sage's breasts. "Who's listening?"

"No. Tell me you aren't wearing a wire." Her father took her by the arms and shook her while her mother ripped open her shirt.

Her mother stripped the device from Sage's body, tossing it to the ground and stomping on it.

Sage tried to heave in a deep breath but couldn't fill her lungs. Her eyes stung as if her lids were sandpaper. Until this very moment, she had still held out hope that maybe, just maybe, her parents still had a grasp on their humanity.

Well, her mother was far from human.

"You stupid girl," her father muttered, shoving her into the island.

Her back arched as she slammed into the hard surface. Her legs buckled, and she fell to her knees. A sharp pain vibrated her teeth.

"Where are they?" her mother said, standing over her, still waving the gun. "How far away?"

"I don't know." Sage found it difficult to take in a full breath. Spots filled her vision, and her stomach gurgled, threatening to empty its contents. She glanced up just as her mother swung her gun across the side of Sage's face. Her body jerked forward, and she landed face-first on the floor. Her head cracked against the white tile.

Sage opened her mouth, but nothing came out. A mirage of colors swirled across her eyes right before it went completely dark.

And silent.

"You can't just barge in there."

Clayton clipped his weapon on his belt loop and glared at Boomer from inside a federal van parked five blocks from the Adams' residence. "Like hell I can't and don't give me any shit about it because we both know if the woman you love were in there, you'd be knocking down the front door."

"Exactly, that's why we need to adjust the plan and move in with our heads on straight."

"My head—and my heart—are exactly where they need to be. Now, I'm jumping that fence and walking through the front door." Clayton held up his hand. He had no desire to listen to Boomer, or anyone else, give him all the reasons why what he was about to do was insane because he didn't care. No way in hell could he sit back and wait. Not when Sage was in danger. "Now, step aside. I wouldn't want to have to hurt you."

Boomer moved to his right, holding his hands up. "I won't try to stop you, but let me go with."

"Yeah," Swede piped in. "We don't know if anyone else is in the house. Dustin is hanging out in a tree near the back. Frost has the far east corner of the property, and I'll go cover the front."

"I'll call for reinforcements as well as hit up all the warehouses and buildings that we know are owned by any of Stanley's companies," Benny said. "We've got your back."

"Thanks." Clayton pulled open the van slider and stepped out into the dark. The cool desert air rolled across his skin like a mountain breeze hitting the valley as day turned into night.

He jogged down the street and was surprised to see the gate to the Adams' estate wide open. Either they never shut it, or they were about to leave.

Or they were expecting him.

Keeping his back to the tree line, he drew his weapon and raced toward the open garage door. He slipped past his truck and then a Porsche. Holding his breath, he gripped the handle and turned slowly. As soon as the door cracked open, he could hear a female voice.

"This is all your fault," a female voice said. "You've always had a soft spot for her and look where it got us."

Clayton inched into the house. He pressed his back against the doorframe into the kitchen. He held his weapon ready as he peeked his head around the corner.

His pulse exploded when his gaze landed on Sage, passed out on the tile floor.

"Look who decided to join us." Lorna Adams stepped in front of him, holding her weapon toward Sage. "And you came alone?"

"My team doesn't have the authority, and the Feds can't do anything since they got nothing on the wire."

"Nothing?" Stanley came into view holding a shotgun. "I find that hard to believe."

"Well, nothing they could use since the wire isn't legal, but I wasn't about to leave Sage with the likes of you two."

"She's our daughter. She'll come around to seeing things our way."

"No, I won't," Sage moaned as she rolled to her side. "What are you doing here?" She blinked a few times.

"Saving your adorable ass." He tried to keep his smile from lighting up his face, but it was impossible to stifle. "How are you feeling?"

"Like my mother just smacked me upside my head with a fucking gun, and that just pisses me off," Sage said.

"I've had enough of this," her mother jabbed her weapon into Clayton's gut. "I pull the trigger, and your guts will be all over the place, and no one will be able to put you back together again."

"You pull the trigger, and I pull mine," Swede's deep voice filled the room.

Clayton didn't need to glance over his shoulder to know his buddy stood five paces to his right.

"And don't get too cute because we've got the front covered as well," Swede said.

"That's right." Boomer made himself visible across the kitchen. "And we've got another man perched in a tree across the street, so the second you try to make a run for it, we gun you down."

Stanley reached down and grabbed Sage by the hair, yanking her to her feet, using her as a shield. A second later, Lorna stood behind both of them, pointing her gun directly at Sage.

Smart woman, because most men wouldn't do anything reckless when their women were at stake.

Then again, Clayton wasn't most men, and while he wanted Sage to be his woman, he'd have to save her first, and that meant taking more than a calculated risk.

"You're going to let us go, or we put a bullet in her head," Stanley said.

"Do it." Sage's eyes narrowed into tiny slits. She shifted her hand, showing a knife.

*That's my girl.*

He blinked twice; hopefully, she understood that he was cool with what he hoped she was thinking and planning.

"He shoots us, and you die," Lorna said.

"A small price to pay for justice," Sage said softly.

"Agreed." Clayton gave Sage a slight nod.

Quickly, she raised her hand and forcefully rammed the knife into her mother's side.

Lorna groaned, dropping her weapon.

*Bang!*

A sharp pain tore through Clayton's side. "Shit," he moaned.

"You are so going to pay for that," Sage said.

Clayton dropped to his knees, holding his side with one hand, his weapon with the other. He focused on Stanley, who held Sage tight to his body.

Boomer raced in and secured Lorna, but Stanley inched closer to the door.

"I'm going to shoot you," Clayton said. "Even if I have to shoot through Sage to do it."

"Right," Stanley said.

"Just do it." Sage nodded, then leaped toward the other side of the room.

*Bang!*

Stanley's arms flapped like a bird as he stumbled backward.

Swede raced into the room.

Clayton collapsed to the floor. Everything around him blurred.

"Clayton," Sage said, cradling his head in her lap. "Stay, still."

"That hurt," he said with a long moan. "But I'd do it again to feel your arms around me once more."

"You're crazy," Sage said.

"I'm crazy in love."

"Now, you're just delusional." She pressed her hand against his wound.

He groaned. "No. I love you, Sage. Tell me you feel the same way."

Her lips brushed against his. "The ambulance is on the way."

"Say it." Fear gripped his vocal cords. His mind faded into a dark place, and he didn't want to die without hearing her say what he knew she felt.

What he felt.

What he wanted and needed more than life itself.

"I need to know how you feel." His breathing had become labored. He could hear his buddies in the background calling out orders. An EMT took over putting pressure on his wound.

Clayton blinked a few times, trying to focus on Sage, and Sage only. "Please, I'm begging."

"You need to save your—"

"I know where this bullet hit. I know I'm mortally wounded. Whether I make it or not is immaterial. I love you, and I need to know if you feel the same way."

She bent over and kissed his lips. "Yes. I love you. Now shut up and let these people do their jobs."

# CHAPTER 11

*THREE WEEKS LATER...*

SAGE PARKED Clayton's pickup truck next to the trailer. She tossed the keys in her purse and dropped that to the ground. Quickly, she went about stacking wood in the firepit. She couldn't bring herself to go in the trailer just yet. Sleeping there alone had proved to be complicated.

Once she got the fire going, she plopped down on one of the folding chairs. She wanted a glass of wine, but that would require her to go inside, and that wasn't something she was ready to do.

For the last three weeks, needing to do something while Clayton recovered in Montana, she'd come to the Alley Home, as well as other shelters and educational centers in the Vegas area and cooked, cleaned, or whatever else was needed. She had wanted to go to Montana, but she had some loose ends she needed to deal with regarding her parents, and Clayton had said he needed to focus, and she'd be a distraction.

She glanced at her phone. Clayton called every evening at six.

It was six thirty.

She contemplated calling him, but she didn't want to come off too needy. Besides, he seemed distant, like he was pulling away. During their last couple of conversations, there were too many long, awkward pauses.

He'd told her that he loved when he thought he'd been dying, and he hadn't repeated those words since.

Because she was no longer lying to herself, she had to admit that hurt, but she shouldn't be surprised. People said all sorts of strange things when they thought they were near their last breath. But it was the last question he asked her yesterday that made her heart heavy.

*Have you taken a pregnancy test?*

When she answered no, Clayton made her promise she'd take one today. Well, she didn't need to take it because she'd gotten her period last night.

She wasn't pregnant, and that would be all he needed to say goodbye to her once and for all.

It was for the best.

The sound of an engine approaching caught her attention. A four-door sedan rolled to a stop about twenty feet away. The rear passenger door opened, and she gasped.

"Clayton?" She stood, smoothing down the front of her jeans.

"In the flesh." He moved slowly toward her. "Surprise," he said with a smile.

Her heart lurched to her throat, and her pulse raced. "You should have told me. I would have come to get you." She bit back a sob that bubbled in her gut. He'd lost a few pounds and walked with a slight limp, but otherwise, he looked like a little piece of heaven.

He held one hand out. "No, hug?"

She swallowed, closing the gap. "I don't want to hurt you."

"Not being able to hold you has been killing me," he said softly, tugging her to his chest. His long fingers threaded through her hair. "God, I've missed you."

"I've missed you too." She rested her head on his shoulder, taking in a deep breath. "Thanks for letting me use your trailer. I've been looking for a place. I haven't been able to find one I can afford yet, but I have a couple of places I can stay."

He took her chin with his thumb and his forefinger. "What the hell are you talking about?"

"You know all of my folks' assets were seized, and my foundation hasn't been cleared yet, and that could take months—"

"Have you read your email today?"

She shook her head. "I volunteered two shifts at the Alley Home today."

He smiled. "Everyone loves you there." He tucked a strand of hair behind her ear. "But you really need to check your email more often. The Feds cleared you and your foundation. You can be up and running anytime you want."

"I need to legally change the name, but I have no idea to what," she mumbled, pushing from his all too familiar embrace.

"I'm sure a name will come to you." He laced his fingers through hers and squeezed. "Did you take the test?" he asked with a hint of a smile.

"You have nothing to worry about. I'm not pregnant." She did her best to keep the utter sadness she felt for something she had never hidden from the only man she'd ever be able to love. Her gaze dropped to her feet. "You are free to move about the country."

"I'm disappointed about the baby too." He cocked his head and ran his thumb over her cheek. "I don't want to go anywhere without you." His lips brushed against hers with a promise of something more. "I'll move back to Vegas if that's what you want, but there is a nice little ranch for sale in Montana right near my friend who works with injured vets. I swear, she's the reason I got upright so fast, and I think what she does might be a good cause for your foundation."

She opened and closed her mouth a half-dozen

times. Her mind rolled his words around because no way could she have heard him correctly.

"You know, I don't expect you to take my name, but now that I'm thinking about it, The Porter Foundation has a nice ring to it, if you want. Or maybe you could call Sage Charities. I like both, but it's up to you."

"Take your name?" she whispered. "Disappointed I'm not pregnant? Buy a ranch?" She pinched the bridge of her nose. "I think I need to sit down." She sucked in a deep breath and fumbled her way back to the folding chair. The fire crackled, and the flames shot toward the sky. Her pulse raced so fast she couldn't tell if the heat she felt on her skin was from the human-made fire.

Or the fire burning in her heart.

Clayton got down on one knee in front of her. "I love you, Sage. I thought you knew that."

"I don't know. You woke up a few days after surgery and were whisked away. Then you asked me to take care of your things and the last few times we talked, it was weird, and you seemed so worried that you could be a father—"

"Oh, babe, I wasn't worried about that. If anything, I was worried you wouldn't want to have a kid with me. But we can keep trying. I mean, most people don't get knocked up first time out of the gate."

"Who are you, and what have you done with Clayton?" She cupped his cheeks. "Are you serious?"

"I'm sorry if I neglected you these last two weeks. I

just wanted to get healthy, so I could come back here and sweep you off your feet."

She slapped his shoulders. "Next time, take me with you so I can be by your bedside. I don't want to be swept away; I want to be part of something."

"Part of a family?"

She nodded. "I want to get married and have kids. And I want that with you. I love you, Clayton."

He shoved his hand in his pocket and pulled out a sparkling diamond ring. "Sage, I love you with all that I am, will you marry me?"

Covering her mouth, she held in the deep sob that smacked into her throat. "Never in a million years did I think I wanted a proposal, much less a ring."

"Well, I never thought I wanted to buy a house, but you need to see this little ranch. The property isn't that big, and the house needs a little work, but we can make it a home. A real home. One that we can have kids in and where you get to watch me grow old while I get to be in love with a younger woman forever."

She took the ring and slid it on her finger. It fit perfectly. "What are we waiting for? Let's hitch up the trailer and go home—to Montana."

# EPILOGUE

*Two Months Later*

"Are you sure you want to do this?"

Clayton stared at the piece of paper in his hands and nodded. "No one has ever called me Porter, so changing my name to Clayton Porter makes perfect sense, especially since you want to rename your not-for-profit to The Porter Foundation."

Sage waved her ring under his nose. "Don't forget that I'm changing my name to Sage Porter. That way, everyone in our little family will have the same last name, and there won't be any confusion." She took his hand, kissed his palm, and then placed it on her stomach. "Today marks the first day of the rest of our lives."

"Well, all we have to do is sign on the dotted line, stand before a judge, and say I do." He went to take a step back, but she pressed his hand firmly against her middle.

"I took the test this morning."

"What test?" he asked as he stared at a single tear that had rolled down her cheek. "Oh." He dropped his gaze to his hand, covering her womb. "A baby?"

She nodded her head wildly. "I thought our wedding day was as good a day as any to tell you."

"Best wedding present a man could ask for." He lifted her off the ground and twirled her around. "I guess I need to get a move on with the addition to the house."

"No rush on that. For the first few months, I want our baby as close to us as possible."

"You're going to be the best mom ever," he said with a throat full of emotion.

"Only because I have you as the father."

He patted his chest in time with his beating heart. For the first time in his life, he felt whole.

*THANK YOU for taking the time to read ROUGH EDGE. I hope you enjoyed it as much as I enjoyed writing it. Please feel free to write an HONEST review.*

THE BUTTERFLY MURDERS

*The Aegis Network*
THE LIGHTHOUSE
HER LAST HOPE
THE LAST FLIGHT
THE RETURN HOME
Coming soon!
THE MATRIARCH

*The Collective Order*
THE LOST SISTER
THE LOST SOLDIER
THE LOST SOUL
Coming soon!
THE LOST CONNECTION

*Special Forces Operation Alpha*
BURNING DESIRE
BURNING KISS
BURNING SKIES
BURNING LIES
BURNING HEART
BURNING BED
REMEMBER ME ALWAYS

*The Brotherhood Protectors*

**ROUGH JUSTICE**

**ROUGH AROUND THE EDGES**

**ROUGH RIDE**

**Coming soon!**

**ROUGH EDGE**

*The Twilight Crossing Series*

**THE BLIND DATE**

**SPRING FLING**

**SUMMER'S GONE**

**WINTER WEDDING**

*Witches and Werewolves*

**LADY SASS**

**ALL THAT SASS**

**Coming soon!**

**NEON SASS**

**PAINTING SASS**

*Boxsets*

**LOVE CHRISTMAS, MOVIES**

**UNFORGETABLE PASSION**

**A NIGHT SHE'LL REMEMBER**

**SWEET AND SASSY IN THE SNOW**

**SWEET AMD SASSY Prince Charming**

*Novellas*

**NIGHTSHADE**

**A CHRISTMAS GETAWAY**

## ABOUT JEN TALTY

Welcome to my World! I'm a USA Today Bestseller of Romantic Suspense, Contemporary Romance, and Paranormal Romance.

I first started writing while carting my kids to one hockey rink after the other, averaging 170 games per year between 3 kids in 2 countries and 5 states. My first book, IN TWO WEEKS was originally published in 2007. In 2010 I helped form a publishing company (Cool Gus Publishing) with NY Times Bestselling Author Bob Mayer where I ran the technical side of the business through 2016.

I'm currently enjoying the next phase of my life...the empty NESTER! My husband and I spend our winters in Jupiter, Florida and our summers in Rochester, NY. We have three amazing children who have all gone off to carve out their places in the world, while I continue to craft stories that I hope will make you readers feel good and put a smile on your face.

*Sign up for my Newsletter*
*(https://dl.bookfunnel.com/6atcf7g1be)*
*where I often give away free books before publication.*

*Join my private Facebook group*
*(https://www.facebook.com/groups/191706547909047/)*
*where she posts exclusive excerpts and discuss all things*
*murder and love!*

Never miss a new release. Follow me on

Amazon:amazon.com/author/jentalty

And on Bookbub: bookbub.com/authors/jen-talty

ORIGINAL BROTHERHOOD PROTECTORS
SERIES

BY ELLE JAMES

# ABOUT ELLE JAMES

ELLE JAMES also writing as MYLA JACKSON is a *New York Times* and *USA Today* Bestselling author of books including cowboys, intrigues and paranormal adventures that keep her readers on the edges of their seats. With over eighty works in a variety of sub-genres and lengths she has published with Harlequin, Samhain, Ellora's Cave, Kensington, Cleis Press, and Avon. When she's not at her computer, she's traveling, snow skiing, boating, or riding her ATV, dreaming up new stories. Learn more about Elle James at www.elle-james.com

Website | Facebook | Twitter | GoodReads | Newsletter | BookBub | Amazon

*Follow Elle!*
www.ellejames.com
ellejames@ellejames.com

f facebook.com/ellejamesauthor
🐦 twitter.com/ElleJamesAuthor